THE CRADLE OF EVIL

EMILY'S KENNEBUNK NIGHTMARE

TIM O'LEARY

Copyright © 2023 Tim O'Leary.

All rights reserved. No part of this book may be reproduced, stored, or transmitted by any means—whether auditory, graphic, mechanical, or electronic—without written permission of both publisher and author, except in the case of brief excerpts used in critical articles and reviews. Unauthorized reproduction of any part of this work is illegal and is punishable by law.

ISBN: 979-8-89031-529-8 (sc)
ISBN: 979-8-89031-530-4 (hc)
ISBN: 979-8-89031-531-1 (e)

Because of the dynamic nature of the Internet, any web addresses or links contained in this book may have changed since publication and may no longer be valid. The views expressed in this work are solely those of the author and do not necessarily reflect the views of the publisher, and the publisher hereby disclaims any responsibility for them.

THE EWINGS PUBLISHING

One Galleria Blvd., Suite 1900, Metairie, LA 70001
(504) 702-6708
1-888-421-2397

CONTENTS

THE CRADLE OF EVIL
–1–

EMILY
–93–

KENNEBUNK
–135–

THE CRADLE OF EVIL

FOREWORD

The characters in the book are mostly new. Emily and Shawn Crawford are long-lasting members of my literary works. The Entity mentioned in the story is a Spirit that guides Shawn through most of his adventures as the latter travels back and forward through time via a portal called The Gateway.

Both Shawn and Emily are Agents of The Entity who orchestrates missions that reflect upon the overcome of Evil by the Good in the world. A lot of what is written is based on fact in terms of the location of the Fort and the houses located toward the Town's center. The French and Indian War played a significant role in the ability of these early settlers in the Township to survive. Hidden compartments behind wood panels did exist for hiding purposes within the homes.

To get a better appreciation of the O'Leary story relating to the supernatural event mentioned in this book, I would invite you to read 'The Narragansett Trail'. I hope you enjoy this short journey into a bit of history relating to the Town of Gorham, Maine. Enjoy the Moment!

CAST OF CHARACTERS

EMILY ROSS: A young girl of twelve years old who possesses special powers given to her by The Entity. She is the modern-day Daughter of Sean and Evelyn Ross.

SHAWN CRAWFORD: An Agent of The Entity and Time Traveler. He is directed to perform mission assignments that involve saving of Presidents formerly assassinated, as well as other well-known and respected personalities who had fallen by an assassin's bullet.

SEAN ROSS: Friend of Tim O'Leary and retired Maine State Trooper. He and his Wife Evelyn live on the southern border of Sebago Lake. The Ross Family live on the Sebago Lake shoreline twelve months a year.

TIM AND LYNN O'LEARY: Residents of the modern Town of Gorham for the past 38 years. Tim is a retired military officer and helicopter pilot. Lynn worked as a real estate agent for 30 years before retiring. They own one of the oldest homes constructed in the late 19th Century.

THE ENTITY: An Inter Galactic Being that directs Agents to interfere and interrupt life events so that the world may live in harmony and peaceful co-existence.

COLETTE: Shawn Crawford's temporal Daughter. Twelve years of age and true Daughter of The Entity. Precocious in her ways and Protector of her father.

PROLOGUE

It had been months since the last 'demon outbreak' in the Gorham, Maine Township. Before that, the Agents of The Entity, Dr. Martin Wesolowski, Emily, Tim O'Leary, and Shawn Crawford had lived without fear of an occurrence that would put their citizens in jeopardy. The last episode happened in the O'Leary's back yard when a Demon dressed in a black cloak challenged Shawn Crawford and others for the right to dominate the small village. The Demon had not been alone. The then current Mayor of Gorham had been in office for more than a decade. No one knew that Mr. Curtis was a shape shifter and had the ability to transform into a massive black hound whenever the Demon wanted him to do so. Two others made up the remaining members of the Demonic Team.

In a final showdown, Shawn and his few allies destroyed the evil group through the use of The Entity's power. The Village was then able to continue its normal everyday business without anyone else in the Town knowing what had transpired that night on Main Street.

And, thus far, tranquility had been the norm. Until, one dark evening on a small island near the Sebago Lake shoreline.

THE CRADLE OF EVIL

The coven of witches, three to be exact, rested on the north side of Sebago Lake. It was a small area of woods on a parcel of land surrounded by the spacious body of water, It was night, 2:06 AM to be exact. There was no wind. Clouds passed slowly by the full moon. To a summer-resident islander, who were only a handful in number, the atmosphere felt evil. A rippling of the nearby water lapping onto the sandy shore projected a sense of pretentious calm. Above such serenity, however, an ominous presence lurked overhead like a blanket ready to fall onto the small patch of land.

Two figures sat opposite one another and faced a five-sided symbol written into the soft sand before them. The third witch, in command of the other two, ambled over in a slow shuffle. They wore hooded dark robes that stretched from head to foot. To see them without their faces covered would have sent a cold chill to any who stood surreptitiously watching the meeting unfold.

"It is time, my Sisters," the Leader croaked. "Prepare yourselves." The other two slowly rose to their feet. The three then held out their hands that were grasped by each of them as they moved toward the sketched symbol before them in the sand. The witches moved closer together each touching the pentagram below with the very tip of their exposed feet. They closed their eyes.

There was a sudden shriek in the air as the wind began to pick up around them. Dark roiling clouds hung directly overhead. Their robes began to flutter about them. The eyes of the three witches suddenly opened and were totally white in color. They peered upward as a dark cloud, like a funnel, dropped downward. It rested five feet above the three. From the mist, a dark-clothed figure materialized and rested itself in the middle of the pentagram.

On the outer periphery of the small clearing, six huge black wolfhounds appeared. They were snarling at the three witches before them. Their eyes were yellow with red tinges of color surrounding their irises. With teeth bared, they slowly approached the witches who were still holding hands. The wind now was howling. The moon had disappeared as if snatched away by an evil entity.

"You have disappointed me!" the Evil One bellowed as it slowly turned and faced each witch from the center of the pentagram. "Must I threaten to destroy all of you for your failures? Do not fail me once more. The consequences of such inability comply with my commands will result in a suffering so great you will rue your very existence!"

The Evil One then looked at the wolfhounds and ordered them to stay where they were. Each of the six stopped their snarling and obediently lay outside the witches' circle. "As I cannot trust that your willingness to do my work is legitimate, I am placing these six hounds with you as an assurance that my wishes are complied with. You have been warned this final time!"

The hounds around the circle moved as one and closer to the witches. "Back away!" the leader of the witches cried out. A hound to the rear of the vocal witch charged her and drove her head first to the ground. She immediately turned over and scurried a few feet using her legs to propel her backward. The hound approached slowly with yellow teeth barred.

"You have lost control, old woman!" the hound snarled as he shape-shifted into a man before her. His eyes were blood red and he showed a large fang on either side of his mouth. The hound turned vampire knelt over the woman and drove his mouth downward onto the side of her neck. The witch shrieked in pain, then dropped her head to the ground and lay lifeless. The other two witches shrank back in fear.

The vampire turned to both of them and said, "There should be no further need for 'discussion' about your willingness to comply with the Master's demands. We will be watching you. Capture the girl, or we will return. Do not fail us!"

The other hounds rose and each snarled at the two women as they trotted past. The two witches stood there together and holding one another. They were trembling in total paralysis. They were left alone in the darkened area as the full moon re-appeared. In the distance, a series of blood curdling howls could be heard across the Sebago Lake area.

GORHAM TOWNSHIP, 1745

The twelve-year-old girl by the name of Emily told her parents that she was going outside the Fort to pick flowers growing near the fortress walls. They warned her to stay close by and to heed the sentries if a warning was given. The Indians in the Narragansett Township had continued their sporadic raids against the settlers still living outside the small Fort located on the northern part of Town. It rested on top of a hillock that offered 360-degree view of the clearing around it, as well as the wood line some 100 meters away on all sides. Within 25 meters from the main gate, there was an out cropping of woods and a small but nearly hidden trail leading to a cluster of homes inhabitant by Town's people who chose the freedom to remain where they lived. They were ever vigilant, for the French and Indian War was far from over for the Native Americans.

    The distance from the Fort to the nearest home was about a quarter-mile to the south. Emily had timed the sentries view of the area, and specifically the nearby trail. Once on this partially hidden dirt path, Emily was shielded from all Fort lookouts. She could then proceed at a leisurely pace to her Friend Sarah's home. The latter's Family was affluent and, in the timber, cutting business. Their home was a two-story wooden structure made of the finest wood and cut to precise specifications. Within, Sarah's Father had hidden compartments installed within the walls. These would afford added protection for all living therein for they were large enough to hide each member of the Family comfortably against overwhelming Indian attacks upon the neighboring properties.

Emily walked slowly along the trail listening to the bird's chatter and stopping every so often to smell a flower or two. She was half-way to Sarah's home when she stopped abruptly in the middle of the trail. There, before her, about ten feet away, sat a huge white hound licking a paw. It briefly looked toward Emily and continued to clean the bottom of its leg. Finally, it sat straight up and looked at the girl for a full 15 seconds. Emily did not move, nor did she show any fear.

The majestic white beast got up slowly and walked toward the stationary girl. It stopped some three feet away and sat down in the middle of the trail. It then shapes shifted into a man over six feet in height. He had sandy colored hair and very light blue eyes. The man wore a one-piece cloth fabric with multiple insignia displayed on its left chest. On the other side, approximately the same length, was a name stitched onto the clothing itself. It read 'Crawford'.

'Hello, Emily," the man said with a wide and crooked grin. "Don't be afraid. I know that you are going over to Sarah's home. Let's just say that now would not be the best possible time to do so. There is an Indian attack pending on the row of homes where Sarah's Family lives. The Indian leader is looking for a particular young girl about your age. You don't have to ask why I know this.

"Sarah and her Family will be safely tucked away in their hidden rooms within the house. The Indians will not torch the home but will take everything they can put their hands on and move on to the next dwelling. It will all be over in less than a minute. When the leader finds no one fitting your description within the building, he will direct his 'associates' to keep looking elsewhere. It will soon be over. There will be loss of life in the small Village, but Sarah and her Family will be safe."

Loud sounds reached both the man and Emily. The girl cringed knowing that the stranger's prediction was occurring. She instinctively moved to the trail's edge and knelt. The tall stranger merely stood and looked toward the screams coming from the center of the Township. Around a small bend in the trail leading to Sarah's home, an Indian suddenly appeared.

He wore war paint on his face and chest. The Indian stopped abruptly and looked at the man and girl standing 30 feet away. Emily instinctively stood behind the tall stranger and waited. Nothing was said. It was akin to a 'future' western standoff. Then it happened.

The Indian shape shifted into a huge black wolfhound, barred its teeth and charged forward. The stranger, almost simultaneously, turned himself back into the great white hound. It was a battle between evil and good. Emily's 'Champion' returned the charge and both 'animals' met with a spectacular collision in mid-air. They both fell heavily to the ground and quickly recovered. The black hound bled from its left ear; the white beast was unaffected by the fierce collision.

At the same moment, both hounds shape shifted back to their human shells. The Indian's right temple was smeared with oozing blood. The stranger peered intently at his enemy. The Indian bared its teeth showing fangs and took a step forward, then stopped.

"Crawford, now is not the time for us to take the girl. You will need much more protection from your worthless Entity before we meet again. For the next time then. I am going to enjoy a taste of your blood when you plead for your life!"

The demon vampire turned quickly and disappeared around the trail leading to the settlement. Crawford turned to Emily to ensure that she was alright. He found her gone from sight. Crawford took a few steps back and toward the Fort. He saw Emily halfway to the gates and running. The sentries immediately noted her distress and called for the gates to be opened. The men then prepared for an attack that never came.

Present Day, Town of Gorham

Tim and Lynn O'Leary owned one of the oldest homes in Gorham, Maine. The original house was built around 1897 on a foundation that remained to this day. The original dwelling burned to the ground circa 1912, but was re-built on the original foundation a year later. It was reputed to be the first house in the Town to receive electricity. It was located on Gorham's outer east Main Street along State Route 25 and across from the Public Safety Building.

The layout of the two-story wooden structure remained constant until the O'Leary's re-modeled their home by putting on an addition to the rear of the existing small two-bedroom dwelling. This occurred in 2003 as Lynn's success as a Real Estate Broker resulted in more than enough income to provide the new inclusive two stories. An in-ground pool was added in 1987 and their old driveway was re-done to add more space for parking to the rear of their single acre-owned land. During that same year, a two-car garage was built toward the end and side of the far end parking area.

    Their Daughter Shelley and Emily were best Friends. During the hot summer months, Shelley insisted that Emily come over and swim in the pool. Both the O'Leary's and Emily's Parents, Sean and Evelyn Ross, had known one another since both girls were born two months apart in 2005. The Ross' welcomed the opportunity to spend an afternoon with Tim and Lynn who usually hosted the get-together with a full-blown barbecue to include hot dogs, hamburgers, chicken and steak. Potato and macaroni salads were always included.

One beautiful summer day on the final day of July, the outside temperature was 85-degrees with a shallow breeze blowing across the property. Tim and Sean sat around the umbrella table and talked about the recent sightings of huge black wolfhounds in and around the Sebago Lake area. Several people had noticed huge shadows lurking around the cabins and lake front areas.

One summer resident believed he actually saw one of the hounds from a short distance away. The way this individual reported the incident to the County Sheriff's Deputy was that the animal was massive and had bright yellowish eyes. He told the Deputy that the hound snarled at the man and immediately bolted across the busy two-lane road skirting the Lake and into the woods.

The 'gentleman' was known to stay up late and was often seen by nosy neighbors 'at the bottle' late into the evening. Sean could only speculate that the 'Lakers' were not taking the man seriously and dismissed the report as one given by a drunkard.

As Lynn and Evelyn sat at a nearby shaded table watching their two daughters enjoy the comfort of the pool water, Tim asked Sean what he believed was going on at the Sebago area. The latter, being a retired Maine State Police Officer, said that he had always been wise not to dismiss any report unless conclusively confirmed or denied. As the Ross Family had a summer 'home' on the southern edge of the Lake, Sean had become ever more vigilant. Together with their German Shepherd named Cody, Sean provided the necessary and prudent security in and around their lake-front property to protect his Family.

"Did you know, Tim, that the Sebago Lake area, and specifically the small islands there, was historically known as the Cradle of Evil. This was a term that sprang up during the 17th Century when the Salem Witch Trials were on-going down in the Commonwealth. It is said that several 'covens' of witches migrated to the Maine area during those times, but nothing could ever be proven that this was true. Only lately, within the past few months have some very strange events have been occurring all around the periphery of the Lake.

"Residents' pets have been found totally torn apart in neighborhood backyards. A horse farm nearby was attacked six weeks ago and one of the colts was found after being dragged off into the woods and grossly mutilated. People around the area are beginning to get extremely nervous and hardly anyone goes outdoors at night. Local Sheriff's Department officials have investigated but have come up empty. Really strange happenings."

"Sean, I have never mentioned this to anyone else before, but we had a supernatural horrific occurrence here at the house last summer. I know you, Evelyn and Emily need to get back, so I'll tell you about it the next time we get together. By the way, what's your tomorrow morning schedule look like?

"I have a brief 30-minute follow-up appointment at Martin's Point in Gorham at 8:00 AM. How about we get together at 9:00 AM down the street at Aroma Joe's?"

'Sounds good to me. Sean, listen, be safe over your way. If there is anything that we can do for you guys, just ask and we'll make it happen, OK?"

"Great, Tim. Thanks for that. Let me tear Evelyn away from Lynn. They always seem to find a myriad of things to talk about, even after seeing one another for only a few days. Tim, thanks for a great afternoon. I'll see you tomorrow at 9:00 AM."

GORHAM TOWNSHIP, 1745

Emily reached the edge of the trail leading to the Fort and slowed to a leisurely pace. The sentries noticed her approach after a minute and waved to her from the top. She waved back and took a deep breath. Better not share my experience with the others, she thought.

When she got within the walls, she was met by her Brother Seth, three years younger than Emily. He, like his sister, was extremely precocious and well learned for a nine-year old. Many of the older men in the Fort would often come to him and ask that he read something on a piece of paper. Seth was always accommodating and very often instructive.

Emily and Seth's parents were considered to be intellectuals. Patrick, the Father, served as the Fort's school teacher for 2-3 hours per day, depending upon the attention span of the few children within the Fort. Mary, the Mother, had some practice as a nurse and helped anyone with a concern about spider bites, bee stings, or a developing fever. She had studied plants extensively and was well familiar with their healing power.

Emily walked over to where her mother was busy applying some ointment to the leg of a little girl. When Mary looked over to her, she smiled and asked how the flower picking went. Emily smiled back and said that the volume or variety of flowers had been scarce. Too much picking around the Fort, she insisted. Mary then told her to get her brother and for both of them to wash up before the evening meal.

Meanwhile, Shawn Crawford walked slowly to the edge of the clearing leading to the Fort. He noted that all were secure within the four walls and turned back toward where his confrontation with the other hound had taken place. Crawford met no opposition all the way to where the trail emptied out into Sarah's back yard.

There was no movement around the wooden building, nor were there any candles burning within the home. Shawn checked to ensure that the way was clear and he slowly walked up and around the house and to the front door. It had been left ajar. He walked inside.

On the wall at the far end of the room, there was an inscription traced on the wall in red. It read, "Your time is over, S.C." Shawn looked left and right and saw nothing but over turned chairs and furniture. And then, a sound from the far wall, or within it. He walked over and stood before a series of ornate panels etched into the main wall in the home's first floor. Crawford gently pushed the side of one of the panels and it slowly opened.

A young girl hidden in the wall began to fall forward. Shawn caught her before she hit the flooring. She was gasping for air. She pointed to two other panels adjacent to hers and whispered hoarsely, "Open!" In the first one, he found a woman who was unconscious and barely breathing. "Mother!" the young girl yelled.

Crawford gently took the woman out of the cramped enclosure and placed her on her back and on the floor. He then went to the second panel and pried the door open. An arrow shaft was in the paneling and embedded completely into the wall. As the wood broke free, Shawn saw the body of a middle-aged man who was pinned entirely with the arrow sticking out of his chest. Crawford checked for a pulse and found none.

The woman was beginning to gain consciousness and called out to the girl. "Sarah? Are you alright? Where's your father?" The girl pointed to the wall where Shawn had pried open the wood to get to the man. The woman's eyes went wide and she began wailing. Her Daughter Sarah wept openly in her mother's arms.

Sarah's mother then looked up into Shawn's eyes and demanded, "Who are you?! And why are you here? Aren't the savages still here? And the one with the blood red eyes, he is gone, isn't he?"

"Yes, Ma'am, he is. You are safe now. I'm going to take you both to the Fort so that Emily's mother can attend to what injuries you may have. Please remain here while I get the wagon from the back." He left the house and found the wagon next to the rear of the building. A plow horse was still attached. He went back inside and helped the woman through the back doorway and into the flat bed of the large four-wheel cart. Sarah jumped in beside her mother.

Crawford jumped on the horse bareback and snapped the reins. The horse and wagon began to move. It took 15 minutes to reach the clearing outside the Fort. Shawn jumped down and took out his holstered weapon and fired a shot into the air. It got the sentries' attention and the gate soon opened and several men began running to the stopped cart. Crawford took the opportunity to move back into the wood line before they cleared the opened doors. He was long gone before two of the men took ten steps forward and onto the trail. Three other men led the horse and wagon the remaining distance and into the Fort. The doors were immediately shut.

PRESENT DAY, TOWN OF GORHAM

The following morning, Tim went over to Aroma Joe's and waited for Sean to arrive. He was anxious to talk about the encounter with the 'former' mayor of Gorham, as well as the three other demons in his backyard several months ago. The shape-shifting Mayor Kenneth Curtis had the entire town mesmerized by his charm for over an entire decade. The demon he wanted to talk about with his friend was the one who was defeated in close combat by Shawn Crawford, a Member of The Entity's inner circle. Of course, he wouldn't mention anything about the Inter Galactic Spirit who protected the weak against all evil using Crawford as his temporal instrument. Sean was a pragmatist, but leaned on the conservative side of what he considered to be scientifically grounded.

It was now 9:15 AM and Sean had yet to appear. Ambulance vehicles came screaming up toward the center of town and turned right onto Route 114 toward Sebago Lake. He asked a nearby coffee shop customer if he knew what was going on, The elderly man said he heard on the news that several Lakers were found mutilated that morning. He knew nothing more than that.

Tim jumped into his 2006 Lexus SC 430 convertible and raced after the emergency vehicles. He prayed that nothing had happened to Sean and his family. After what he witnesses a few months back on his own property, he feared the worst. He arrived at the southern edge of the lake and parked far enough away from the parked Rescue Units so as not to impede what the First Responders were doing. He saw Sean and his family near a Sheriff Department's cruiser. It looked as though the former State Trooper was giving the Deputy more than just a piece of his mind. A short distance farther down the road Tim noticed medical personnel carrying body bags to the rear of one of the ambulances.

As the lead person was carrying the last human remains, his hand slipped and one side of the bag opened. It exposed the head of the deceased. Tim cringed as he saw the face of a woman, or thought to be a woman for its entire head was covered in blood.

Before the handler could recover the side of the bag he was holding, Tim saw the eyes open in the mutilated head. They looked directly at him with an all-knowing look. The lips creased in a brief smile before the fiery red eyes closed for good. A chill went up Tim's spine as he watched the body disappear into the rear of the vehicle.

He walked over to where Sean was finishing his tirade toward the Deputy. The latter appeared flustered from the 'conversation' mostly conducted by Sean Ross. Finally, the Deputy turned away and walked over to where the medical personnel were getting ready to leave the area.

"Are you folks, OK?" Tim asked.

'Oh, hi, Tim. Didn't see you standing over there. Yes, we're all fine. Had some pretty gruesome things happen overnight. Two out-of-state renters were found dead outside their lake-side cabins about 8:50 AM. A woman walking her dog found them propped upside down against their dwelling's wall. Their feet had been nailed to the wood.

"One of the victims was a woman in her early 30s; the other a man in his 40s. Their heads had been savagely torn open. Medical personnel on the scene told me that there were huge puncture marks on the side of their necks.

Curiously, there was a small black cat lying on the grass immediately in front of them. It had a white patch on its chest, much like a 'batman' logo. When Rescue arrived, it sat up, hissed, and ran into the woods across the street. One of the men getting out of the vehicle said that he felt a brief chill in the air as the animal reached the far side, turned around and looked at him."

"What was going on with you and the Deputy?" Tim asked.

"The officer and I have an adversarial relationship. He was at the Maine State Police Academy with me going through training. He didn't make it through the program and blamed everyone else for his failure to complete the course. He and I had had a run in at some point during the field training exercise. The man has yet to let it go."

"That's too bad. Listen, why don't you, Evelyn and Emily come over and spend the afternoon with Lynn and me at the pool? We'll cook up some sausage and burgers and just chill out. What do you think? It might help change the mood."

"Tim, I do think that we'll take you up on it. How about we come over a little after noon time. I'll bring the beer."

"Sounds good. I'll head back to the house and let Lynn know that you're coming over. We'll see you all in a little bit."

By this time, all medical personnel had left the area in their vehicles with the victims securely tied down to their gurneys in their body bags. The standard looking ambulance never made it to the hospital. Late that afternoon, it was found on Huston Road in Gorham at the Maintenance Facility. The two medical individuals in the front cabin were found dead at the scene. Each man's head was severed completely. One was placed on the hood of the vehicle facing outward. The other head was nailed to the back door of the vehicle, again facing forward. The bodies were nowhere to be found.

When the ambulance was found by a maintenance crew returning to the pit to replenish material for road repair, they saw it sitting in the middle of the parking lot. The driver, the Town Maintenance Supervisor, got out of his dump truck and walked toward the other vehicle. He stopped short about 50 feet from it and his jaw dropped and eyes went completely wide. He fumbled for his radio switch and immediately called in to the Police Department.

Cruisers began arriving five minutes later. Altogether there were four units responding. Another ambulance from Westbrook arrived ten minutes later. When the neighboring town of Westbrook's personnel arrived, its personnel approached both ends of the Gorham vehicle. One individual opened the side passenger door and was startled by a small black cat with a white fur patch on its chest. It was sitting on one of the headless bodies. The cats' eyes were blood red. It leapt at the EMT's head and began biting the woman's face and neck. After being thrown off by the Technician, the cat raced toward the back of the pit and disappeared into the woods. Moments later, a second neighboring medical unit arrived from the Town of Standish. It would be several hours before everyone had departed the area.

The woman EMT was looked at by another Technician. There were two tiny holes on the side of her neck. She begged off any treatment and continued to assist the others in recovering the remains. When the scene was cleared, the ambulance carrying the decapitated bodies drove away and toward the Maine Medical Center in Portland.

GORHAM TOWNSHIP, 1745

Early the next morning following Sarah and her mother being taken to the Fort for medical care, Shawn's white hound appearance made itself known to the sentries manning their stations. A shout by one of the men got the attention of several more and the gate opened. Emily at a distance followed three men with muskets as they moved cautiously toward the great white beast. The huge hound proceeded to lie down as in a subservient manner.

The girl immediately recognized the beast and darted quickly ahead of the lead man. 'Emily!" he shouted. "Stop! Stop!" Emily continued on and reached the hound and stood over it smiling. She knelt down by its side and hugged the animal. The white beast responded by licking Emily's face.

"Emily, step away now!" the leader demanded.

"No, I shall not," she replied vehemently. "This hound protected me yesterday when I was outside the Fort. I will not let you hurt him!" she said as she hugged the hound's neck firmly. Quietly speaking, Shawn whispered to her, "Emily, not too much on the hugging, OK? I can barely breathe, brave girl."

She looked down at the animal, lightened her hugging, smiled and kissed the hound's head. The men stared at the girl in wonder.

"Come along, Shawn," Emily coaxed. "We're going to officially adopt you in the Fort." She got up and looked at the tall men before her. "Yes, I've named him Shawn. He is my Friend and Protector. Now, let us pass and go into the Fort." Emily walked toward the tall wooden fortress with the great white beast following closely behind. The men parted before her and gave 'Shawn' a wide berth. They looked at one another, shrugged and followed the small girl, and huge white animal into the Fort.

When the white hound entered through the gates behind Emily, everyone took a step back. Several of the men picked up their muskets and started to bring them at the 'ready'. Emily stopped and shouted, "There is no need to fear this animal. It protected me by fighting off one of the Indians while I was outside the Fort. Please, put down your weapons!" She then went to 'Shawn' and wrapped her arms around 'his' neck.

"Not too tight, Emily," Crawford whispered in her ear. She released his neck and told the 'animal' to sit. Shawn obediently complied. Several of the other children, including her Friend Sarah came over to the great white hound.

Shawn looked up at Sarah and said quietly, "Hello, Sarah, I'm glad that you are alright." Sarah took a step back and looked at the hound. She looked at Emily who reassured her friend that everything was alright and that she would explain what she just heard a little later.

Emily shared her story with everyone in the Fort. It was about how this great white hound intercepted an Indian who was about to attack her. There were many questions asked of Emily. Where did the hound come from? Why did it happen to appear just when she was in danger? And, why did it protect Emily against the advancing savage? Shawn just lay there and sighed heavily. I'll bet The Entity set me up for this.

Finally, Emily's mother told everyone that there enough questions for the moment. Emily was told to clean herself up and to be ready to help her mother with providing care to the needy within the Fort. Emily told Shawn to stay with her. He did so but was wary of anything happening out of the ordinary, both outside and within the Fort's walls. That afternoon, Shawn was treated to scraps of food left over by the settlers. It doesn't get any better than this, he thought.

During the late afternoon hours, he noticed one individual man appearing to be extremely agitated about something. As Emily had gone down for a brief nap before dinner, Shawn unobtrusively followed the individual to his sleeping area. When the man entered, Shawn walked slowly up to the entrance and dropped down to the ground, feigning sleep. What his ears picked up from inside caused an alarm to go off in his head.

He picked up a voice within quietly chanting something. Shawn low crawled a bit further and was able to peer inside. There was just enough light within that Crawford was able to make out a strange symbol drawn into the ground. The man's eyes rolled back into his head as he nearly toppled backward onto the flooring. The symbol, representing a pentagram, began to glow ever so softly. From the symbol on the ground came a hoarse voice that said, "Tonight!"

Shawn got up and trotted back to Emily's area, stopping only to be pet by a couple of the children.

He played his act fully by nudging against the legs of one of the boys. Shawn then moved on to where Emily was napping and drank some water from a crude bowl that was left for him. He stretched out and waited for darkness.

Two hours later, the man came out of his sleeping area and looked around. No one was in sight. There was something different about this individual. Shawn had crept over during the past five minutes from Emily's area and waited behind an old barrel. This wasn't the individual Crawford had seen hours before. His eyes were bright red and he wore a black cloak. An ebony staff was in his left hand. A live-in Demon within the Fort?

Shawn followed it from a short distance as it walked slowly over to the Fort's gates. Sentries above were unaware of its presence as they focused their attention outward and toward the wood line. The Demon approached a ladder leading to the top of the Fort where two look outs were quietly talking with one another.

Crawford shape shifted back into his human form. He raised both arms forward and a very thin light blue bolt shot forward and struck the figure in the back of the head. The Demon's body forcefully hit the Fort wall beside the ladder and it crumpled to the ground. Immediately, the body decomposed into a mound of ash. Not a sound was heard by anyone.

Shawn then went to the gates, opened one door and skirted the Fort's wall without being seen by the sentries above, He made it to the closest part of the wood line and disappeared from view. After walking for a couple of minutes, Crawford was knocked to the ground from behind.

He quickly turned himself over and saw a huge bat-like animal rise into the night sky. It circled him twice before it landed on the trail 5 meters in front of him. The creature shape shifted into human form. It wore 21st Century clothing and carried a cane. The man began walking toward Crawford. His face was chalk white and he possessed demonic eyes, more like that of a vampire. This characterization was confirmed when the individual smiled exposing two fang-like teeth.

"Ah, Mr. Crawford, or should it be 'Sir Shawn'," the vampire said in a soothing tone. "Yes, yes, don't be surprised that I know you, As a matter of fact, all of my 'brothers' know you all too well. Your 'knighthood' conferred by the Government of Australia was an impressive moment for you, wasn't it? And how is your Wife Christine, Sir Shawn? I wager that she misses you terribly. It's a shame that she is about to lose her husband tonight."

The demonic form floated rapidly toward Crawford and threw the latter to the ground. It turned Shawn's head to the side and was about to bite down on his neck when it was thrown off of his body with a violent force. It fell through the air and hit the ground hard some three feet away. It shrieked in protest; shape shifted back into the bat-like bird and rapidly flew off into the night.

Shawn was still reeling from being knocked to the ground. When he opened his eyes, he saw Emily standing over him. She had a concerned look on her face, but then smiled down at Crawford once she knew he was alright.

'Emily?" he said, "What are you doing here outside the Fort? Shouldn't you be back inside sleeping? And, what happened to the beast that attacked me?"

"My, my, Sir Shawn. I thought I had a lot of questions earlier today. Look at you. You're usually the one with all of the answers," she mocked. "Are you alright, Shawn?"

'Yes, Emily. I'm good. You've got to get back to the Fort. I can escort you to the wall. And, by the way, I'm covered in this light blue residue of some kind. I suspect you haven't lost your 'touch' using The Entity's weapon. There isn't a dry cleaner nearby, is there?"

"Shawn, we're in the 18th Century. The nearest 'dry cleaners' is the stream bed with nearby rocks to beat your wet clothing into some semblance of getting dry. Don't worry about chaperoning me back. There will be no further attacks this evening, both outside and within the Fort itself. I do believe The Entity requires your services. Look above you, Shawn".

Crawford glanced skyward and saw a blue mist descending toward him. It quickly enveloped Shawn and a moment later he was no longer there. The mist dissipated leaving only a trace of a man's impression upon the earth.

Emily turned and found her way back to the Fort without being seen.

PRESENT DAY, TOWN OF GORHAM

The ambulance carrying the mutilated bodies from the Gorham Maintenance Facility made it as far as the Shaw Brothers Construction Site located on Maine State Road 237. It was parked behind one of the sand pits and found by a Shaw Brothers Administrative Assistant approximately 10 minutes after departing the Gorham site. The individual wondered by a medical vehicle was stationary on the property and then noticed blood on the windshield. He called 911 and the Gorham Police responded with several cruisers. This time a

Gorham Medcue Ambulance arrived on the scene moments following the arrival of the Police. As two of the Gorham Officers had been at the scene of the previous discovery of mutilations, the day was wearing very thin.

When one of those Officers checked the front area of the Ambulance, he found one severed head impaled to the headrest on the driver's side. The accompanying female EMT on the passenger side was missing. In the rear of the Ambulance, there were no body bags that carried the two previous First Responders from the Lake area. The Officer noticed a black cat looking at him from a mound of sand 15 meters away. The animal hissed and bolted away and out of sight.

The two EMTs from Gorham placed the severed head in a separate bag from the body. Other than this one victim found there, no one investigated the vehicle any further. Each Officer on the scene was told to stand by the Ambulance and wait for the Maine State Police Criminal Investigation Division and members of the State Forensic Team. They arrived 45 minutes later. By this time, the day was only half over. Only one Gorham cruiser left the scene and that was to follow the Ambulance the remainder of the way to the Maine Medical Center.

Sean, Evelyn, and Emily arrived at Tim's home a little after 12:30 PM. Evelyn was still shaken up over the nightmare in the Sebago Lake area that morning. Emily and Shelley were 'immune' to the tragedy in Emily's 'backyard.' They playfully swam in the O'Leary pool while Sean, Evelyn, Lynn and Tim talked quietly about what had happened that morning.

"I mentioned to you, Tim, about the goings on in the area during the recent past. In my 23 years of Law Enforcement, I have never seen anything as gruesome as what happened this morning. It has people all along the Lake shore on edge, and I can't say that I blame them. Mutilated animal bodies and then this this morning. Renters have begun to pack up and leave for home. This is all incredible!"

"Sean, remember that I had a story to tell you about a 'supernatural happening' that Lynn and I experienced several months back? Well, here is the story, believe it or not."

Tim then recounted the encounter with a Demon and three shape shifters, two incredibly large wolfhounds and an Indian resurrected from the 1744 Gorham Township conflict during the French and Indian War. A doctor, young girl, a time traveler, and an inter galactic presence all coming together to defeat that evil group were able to stop them from turning the Town into one hell of a nightmare. Tim asked if he noticed that a new Mayor of Gorham had been voted into office. Sean said that he had and found it unusual for civic government to take such an action. Tim answered that the then Mayor was a shape shifter and was in collusion with the Demon to take over every aspect of Town politics. Sean looked at Tim and Lynn with an askance look and fell silent for several moments.

"Sean," Tim said, "Come with me. I want to show you something."

They both out to the clearing behind Tim and Lynn's property and approached an old barn that was in dire need of repair. Tim opened the door and asked Sean to step inside with him. On the dirt flooring in the center of the structure was a pentagonal shape seared into the ground. "This where the 18th Century resurrected himself at the beckoning of the Demon."

Sean knelt down and touched one of the symbol's lines. He pulled his hand away immediately and shook it as though he had touched something too hot. He looked up at Time who merely nodded in the affirmative. They both left the barn and proceeded back to the pool area where the girls were continuing to have the time of their lives splashing one another in the shallow end of the pool. Sean was silent all the way back.

"Tim, you mentioned that there was a 'team' that stopped Evil from taking hold in the Village. A girl, you said. Do you remember her name?"

"Sean, it was Emily." Tim looked toward the pool and then back at Sean. The latter stood looking at his friend for a very long moment.

"Tim, we have more to tell one another," Sean said to his friend.

GORHAM TOWNSHIP, 1745

For a reason known only to Emily, she was not disappointed to find 'Shawn' gone in the morning. The talk within the Fort was concerning the missing settler and the curious mound of ash located by the entrance to the Fort. None of the sentries on watch that evening remembered seeing anything out of the ordinary. Several of those within the Fort had known the elderly man for a while and considered him eccentric. Probably wandered off into the early morning sunshine and would reappear in short order. Emily knew better.

During these early morning summer hours, a coven of witches that had migrated from the Salem area down in the Commonwealth had begun to establish themselves on a small island that was very close to the main shore of Sebago Lake. During the day they represented old spinsters that knit wool into blankets and sweaters. They were often seen on the mainland by several of the few inhabitants in the area. What was curious was that no one could figure out how they got from the small patch of land to the shore. No boat was visible anywhere. Their goods were of very high quality so no one thought more about their mode of transportation. It was none of their business.

In the evening, from the shoreline, one could just make out a whisper of smoke rising from the land's middle area. Again, the smoke was unobtrusive, and no one bothered to question what was going on in the middle of the night. Although, on rare occasions, a howl was heard coming from that small little island. It wasn't a constant occurrence and the locals chalked it up to a wandering coyote.

On this one particular night, the one where Sean interceded within the Fort by eliminating the demonic presence, the witches were extremely agitated. There were three altogether and the leader was pacing back and forth around their small fire they had put together in their clearing. She was extremely fearful that the 'Demon' would arrive with its hounds and more than admonish them for the failure of their Fort Agent from bringing the girl Emily to them. One of the women turned to the side and thought she noticed a set of yellowish eyes looking at them from the nearby brush. She immediately felt chilled to the bone.

"Agnes," the leader said, "What is the matter with you? Are you hallucinating again?"

"No, Mother, I was distracted by some movement in the woods over there. It really is nothing."

Agnes continued her furtive looks away from the fire and almost tuned out the tirade the leader of the coven was exhibiting. Finally, the Leader, Maleficent, stopped and turned toward the shadows some 10 feet away. She began to tremble with fear.

A single black cloud occurred suddenly above them. The witches as one bent downward at the knees and waited. On either side of the woods a huge black hound appeared. They were snarling and snapping their jaws at the women. The mist descended in the middle and atop the fire. It immediately went out. From the blackness materialized a hooded figure who stood before the witches. Its eyes were fiery red and it bared its teeth to show two huge fangs at each corner of its mouth. It looked at each woman with penetrating eyes before speaking.

"Melificent, you have failed me. I am disappointed in your ploy to use that useless agent of yours within the Fort to bring the girl to me. You are no longer needed. However, I will spare you this time, but I am placing Judith in charge of you all from this moment. I want results!" he bellowed. And with that, he was gone, as were his huge wolfhounds.

The former leader could not stop shaking in fear. The other two witches had tears streaming down their faces. And so, the cycle began in the quest to capture the girl for the following two hundred seventy-two years. Each attempt failed and, as a consequence, witches were punished by experiencing horrific results for their ineptitude. For a witch to be identified as a leader in the coven meant almost certain doom. For, Emily, the everlasting 12-year-old girl was a constant, and an Agent of The Entity.

Present Day, Town of Gorham

The next morning, the news about the strange deaths of the Sebago Lake residents and the EMT medical personnel were splashed across the Portland Press Herald. Most Police Officers on the scene were prohibited from speaking about the incidents. However, one Officer was so traumatized after witnessing the human gore created that he gave a clandestine and off-the-cuff account of what he witnessed the day before. The reporter's source was not identified and the newspaper ran the story anyway.

This set-in motion a panic among those living around Sebago Lake. Most summer residents packed up and left for their homes in Massachusetts, New Hampshire and Vermont. Year-round home owners remained, but took great effort in adding to the safety and welfare of themselves and their families by purchasing fire arms and installing multiple locks on their doors of entry. These measures were to no avail as no one really knew or understood the threat facing their tiny community.

Emily pleaded with her mother to let her stay a little longer to swim. After negotiations were concluded, Sean and Evelyn allowed her to stay an additional hour. Tim said that he would gladly take Emily back to Sebago Lake before too long. Sean said that he appreciated the gesture, but that it was not necessary. He and Evelyn would be back to pick Emily up. They were planning on getting a Pizza up the street at the Gorham House of Pizza. The Owner Angelo had promised them each a free meal in celebration of the up-coming wedding of his Son George in three weeks.

After Sean and Evelyn left for Sebago Lake moments later, Tim heard a helicopter approach from the southwest. The sound of the main rotor turbine system grew louder and louder. Tim thought that it couldn't be more than a couple of hundred feet above ground level. He finally spotted it above a tree line a couple of hundred meters away and coming right at his home.

It passed over the house and did two circular patterns around the building. The modified Bell 206J began its approach to Tim's croquet lawn just behind the house. It approached and landed from a high hover over the three tall willow trees at the edge of the development's grass line behind Tim's home.

When the aircraft had taken its two-minute shut down procedure, the main rotor slowly came to a stop. The left cabin door opened and a man in a blue flight suit step out of the aircraft. Tim recognized the pilot and went over to him with a huge smile on his face. On the passenger side of the aircraft, a young girl of 12 years of age, jumped down to the ground and followed the pilot over to where the O'Leary's were standing.

"Shawn, how the devil is you? And, what brings you back to our humble mansion?" he asked. "And is the Colette we've heard so much about?"

"Hey, Timmy. It's good to see you again. Yes, this is my 'Jailer' from the future! She insisted on coming to meet you and Lynn. Colette flew most of the way here. You should see her do barrel rolls in the F-193B Leopard Advanced Fighter."

"Colette, it's finally great to meet you. We've heard so much about you and Christopher. How are your Mother and Brother doing?"

"Mother and Christopher are both well. They wished they could have made this trip through The Gateway. Mr. and Mrs. O'Leary, I've heard a lot about you both as well. I'm glad I had an opportunity to come with Father. He has the greatest amount of respect for you both."

"Thanks for that Colette. I'm not altogether positive that I rate such praise from your Father, but let me say that it is a mutual admiration society we have going. Would you like to join Emily and Shelley in the pool?"

"Yea, baby!" And off she went to join the other two girls. Shawn just raised an eyebrow and said, "She takes after her Brother. So how are you two?"

"We're all well despite the horrible events that happened in the past 24 hours out at Sebago Lake. Let me guess, my Friend, you are here because of those terrible murders and the macabre findings inside local ambulances yesterday."

"And, how is Emily doing?" Shawn answered by dodging the question.

"Does she still carry the Amulet with her?"

"Emily is as sweet as ever. And yes, she still has the Amulet and keeps it quite safe by the way. The power ability of that small piece of metallic substance is truly incredible."

"Yea, Tim, we're going to need that ancient medallion if we're going to clean up some loose ends that we didn't take care of here at your home a few months back."

"Come on in and have a cup of coffee with me and Lynn. She's been painting the side of the house for the past three weeks and this is a good time for her to take a break."

They walked over to where Lynn was putting another coat of paint on a panel of wood. She looked up and beamed when she saw Shawn. Lynn dropped everything and came over and gave Shawn the biggest hug and a peck on the cheek.

"Hello, Stranger," she said with a big smile. "How are Christine, Christopher and Colette?"

"They're all well, Lynn. Thanks for asking. Christopher is speaking at a science symposium being held in Boston today. Christine is on a routine flight in the F-193B Leopard Advanced Fighter. She took off from the Sydney Maritime Base about two hours ago. As for Colette, turn around and look over in your pool area. I sense that she is having a great time with Emily and Shelley by the sounds of splashing and things."

Lynn then spotted Colette, a beautiful 12-year-old playing a game of 'hover'. She was actually prone to the surface of the pool water, but 12 inches above it. Colette looked completely at ease and encouraged the other two girls to join her on her 'air mattress'. Amazingly, Emily while lying on her back rose up above the water level and lay hovering next to Colette. They both had their hands behind their heads and just lay there. Shelley, who was clairvoyant and was known to speak with the 'dead', tried it and got six inches above the surface before she did an inverted 'belly flop' into the pool.

"Shelley, remember the concentration method I talked to you about. Much of what I spoke about is 'letting go' and not thinking about it. Let The Entity's force flow through you, Shelley. Now, try it again, girl!" Emily insisted.

Shelley made another attempt and assumed a peaceful serene look on her face. In a flash, she rose up, and up, and up, until she was 15 feet above the other two girls. Both Emily and Colette giggled.

"Shelley, shall we say too much exuberance and concentration? I think you have it down cold now. It's tempering your thoughts. Well done, girl. Now come on down and join us."

Sean stood there with his mouth open. His daughter and two friends were above the pool water and floating while talking 'girl stuff'. Sean looked at the other three who merely shook their heads and shrugged at the same time. "May The Entity's force be with you, Sean," Tim mocked with a huge grin. "Coffee, anyone?"

As they went up the deck stairs to enter through the house living room, Shawn turned to Colette and said, "Ease up on the instruction, OK, Colette? I don't want to hear from the FAA in Portland that a 737 airliner on an approach to the airport spotted three girls doing cart wheels in the air over Cape Elizabeth. You're in charge, Sweetheart."

"Yes, Father," Colette replied by rolling her eyes and then giggled.

Shawn just shook his head and walked inside to join the others already seated at the dining room table. "Now, where were we?" he said with a grin on his face.

Shawn sat down on a dining room chair and looked at both Tim and Lynn pensively. After a moment, he said, "It's really good to see both of you again. How long has it been now? Four, Five months? When that 'exercise' was over, I didn't think we'd be meeting again like this to discuss another demon issue."

"I'm certain you've heard through The Entity grapevine that Several EMTs were mutilated while driving their ambulances from scenes of horror. The one common denominator, I've heard about, is that there was a black cat with a white fur patch on its chest at each location. Given everything that has happened, I believe we are dealing with more shape shifters, hounds, vampires, and your 'common' black cloaked demon. I'm glad you're here, Shawn. We need a strategy to overcome what has already become supernaturally unmanageable. Thank 'heavens' for his Blueness sending in the cavalry."

"Tim, we've been seeing what's been going on. We also know that everything is going to come to a head this evening. I understand that Emily's 'Parents', Sean and Evelyn, have returned to their home on the Lake. We have to have them come here tonight."

"They're coming back for Emily in less than an hour from now," Tim answered. "I'm not sure what to tell them to stay here in town after they've up the street for a Pizza dinner."

"Leave that to me, Timmy. In the meantime, you do still have that guest bedroom upstairs, right?"

"Sure do, Shawn. But I'm afraid it would only accommodate one family."

"Tim, no need to think about Colette and me. This will be over tonight and we will be gone before morning," Shawn said.

"What can I do to help out, Shawn?"

"Not a thing, my friend. Together with Colette, Emily and me, we'll have everything taken care of shortly after midnight. Now, do you still have that famous Allagash White in the fridge?"

Thirty-five minutes later, Sean and Evelyn stopped by the house to pick up Emily. "Hope this hasn't been too much of a hassle for you and Lynn, Tim/"

"No, not at all Sean. Let me introduce you to an old friend of mine, Shawn Crawford. He's the Pilot of that Jet Ranger parked out back. Shawn, meet Sean Ross and his Wife Evelyn."

"It's a pleasure to meet you, Mr. Crawford."

"Likewise, Mr. and Mrs. Ross. My Daughter Colette and I flew in from the Hartford area to catch up with these old friends of ours. My Daughter Colette, wait, here she is now. Colette, please meet some friends of the O'Leary's, Mr. and Mrs. Ross, Emily's Parents."

"Mr. and Mrs. Ross, it's my pleasure completely. We've had a lot fun getting to know Emily in this very brief period of time. She's fantastic!"

Well, thank you, Colette. That's very nice to hear. Emily, please change up so that we can go over to Angelo's to have that Pizza you've been talking about all week," Evelyn said. "Right away, Mother," Emily answered with a brief look to Shawn.

While she was changing, Shawn mentioned that there was a lot of news concerning the Sebago Lake area. He hoped the Ross' would be alright given the latest set of occurrences.

"We'll be fine, Mr. Crawford. I'm thinking it's just a flurry of temporary events. We should be fine from this point on. Tim, thanks very much for having Emily stay the extra time. I hope she wasn't a bother," Sean said as Emily came out of the room nearby.

"Hey, Sean and Evelyn, it's always a great pleasure having Emily with us. Let's plan on getting together tomorrow morning, Sean, for the coffee at Aroma Joe's that we missed this morning."

"I'll look forward to it, Nine o'clock still, OK?"
"Great, we'll see you then. Be safe tonight."

After the Ross' had left, Shawn, Colette and the O'Leary's sat down at the kitchen table. Shelley, who had come in earlier from the pool and changed, said that she had a few items to attend to upstairs. She told Colette to come up when she had a chance. The latter said she would be there in a few moments.

Shawn then outlined his plan to destroy the evil that lurked in the Lake area.

Sebago Lake, That Evening

What few Lake Renters that decided to stay in the area, the night time came all too suddenly, given the past day's events. New locks had been installed, pets had been kept indoors and the handful who possessed firearms were prepared for anything. The 'anything' they envisioned was far from their known reality.

The Ross' left the Gorham House of Pizza by 8:00 PM and arrived at their home on the Lake a half hour later. Cody, their German Shepherd, had been left indoors and was eager to see them when they walked through the door. Sean, given his State Police background, made certain that all avenues of entry were secure for the evening. It was 10:30 PM.

Out on the opposite side of the Lake, on a small patch of land close to the shoreline, a howl from an animal was heard. The Sheriff's Department had assigned one of its Deputies to patrol the entire lake front until 6:00 AM the following day. The Officer was sitting in his cruiser and sipping on a coffee he had picked up from Dunkin' Donuts in Standish prior to his drive over to the Lake. As he was thinking of a whole lot other things, he could be doing other than baby-sitting a bunch of Lakers, his car lurched forward suddenly. He looked in his rear-view mirror and thought that some drunk had rear ended him. What he saw chilled him to the bone.

He fumbled with his car radio to report in to the dispatcher. He hadn't got a word out when his door was ripped opened. The Deputy shrieked in terror as a very dark and tall figure dressed in black bent forward and bit into the side of his neck. His body quivered for some 10 seconds before it went limp. The dark-clothed figure backed off and stood looking toward the north end of the Lake. Six huge black hounds bolted out of the shadows and sat quietly around the figure. With a huge ebony staff "Go!" he commanded and they ran off toward the Lake front homes.

Meanwhile, on the small patch of land on the opposite side of the Lake, two witches shape shifted into huge flying bat-like beasts. They flew rapidly toward the Vampire and lighted a few feet from it. The being's blood red eyes turned in the direction of the Ross' property. It raised its staff held in its left hand and pounded it heavily into the sandy shoreline. The beasts lifted into the air and flew the very short distance to the Ross' property where they stood cackling and salivating.

Inside the Ross home, Cody began growling incessantly. Finally, he began barking and baring his teeth while facing the front door. Sean Ross tiptoed into the foyer and knelt down beside the huge

German Shepherd. He pets the dog on the back and quietly told him to sit. Cody did so while still showing his large sharp teeth and growling at the closed front door.

About this time, a Toyota Prius pulled up on the opposite side of the Ross' lawn. Shawn and Colette exited the vehicle and started walking toward the front of the home. One of the bat-like beasts threw itself against the front door of the home and nearly knocked it off its hinges. The other took to the air, circled both Shawn and Colette, and dove toward them.

Colette stood resolutely and waited for the right moment. When the flying beast was inches above her face, she reached up and grabbed its neck just behind the creature's head and squeezed tightly causing the large maw to open widely. With the other hand, she pulled from her pocket a light blue metallic object and pushed it down the beast's throat. Colette then let go of the witch and it flew off into the night. Moments later, a huge muffled explosion shattered the tranquility of the Lake. The beast had swallowed a very small box-like object with a timer infused into the material. When the explosion occurred, human and bat-like entrails fell to the ground over a small area.

The other witch rammed the door a second time and the wooden portal shattered completely. It walked inside and stood face to face with the girl Emily, Sean Ross, and the Shepherd. Cody started barking nonstop. Sean grabbed his 9 mm service weapon and started firing rounds point blank into the monster. The bullets had no effect.

"Father, please stop shooting. Trust me that I will have all of this back to normal in a few seconds. Do not stop me, Father." She quickly turned toward the beast and pulled out a metallic object from her pajama pocket. Emily pointed the Amulet toward the slowly advancing bat-like beast. Cody was being held back by Sean who was pleading with Emily to top immediately.

The young girl levitated from the floor and stopped six feet in front of the beast. Her body was outlined in a clear coat of light blue mist. Emily's eyes were also light blue and piercing. Cody was barely being restrained by Sean at this point.

The beast opened its mouth and spewed forth a dark red liquid substance directed at Emily. As soon as it struck the light blue veil surrounding the girl, it disintegrated into red ash. The horrific creature went into a rage. Emily remained in a hover mode and moved closer to the beast. The Amulet, still held before her, began to glow a copper color. It was very warm to the touch.

The girl reached out and touched the creature's chest with the Amulet. The copper Medallion turned gold-colored and emitted a razor-sharp bolt of pure energy through the beast. It began convulsing while shrieking loudly in pain. In less than five seconds, it was propelled backward and onto the lawn in front of the shattered door. It writhed in horrible pain. Emily walked out through the framework where a door once stood and approached the dying beast. She took the Amulet and pointed it at the creature's head. Once again, a light blue bolt shot forward and struck the head causing it to explode.

Emily immediately turned toward her father and Cody who were now silently watching the girl levitate back into the house. When her feet touched the floor, she kissed him on the cheek and said, "Father, I have much to explain to you. But it will have to wait. Please remain here with Cody. I am going to help Shawn and Colette rid this area of everything evil. This home will not be attacked ever again. Please see that Mother is OK inside the house. I will soon be returning."

She disappeared before Sean.

Shawn had walked slowly over to the next property where the black-cloaked demon stood watching his approach. Crawford stopped six feet in front of the monster who towered over Shawn by several inches. They stood looking at one another before the demon said, "You are dying tonight, Shawn Crawford." The demon's hounds then materialized around the vampire.

"Don't think I am going to be the one leaving no longer breathing, Dirt bag," Shawn countered. "There is going to be death tonight, and it is going to be you and your minions being sent back to hell. How can you be even associated with these weak-looking 'puppies' of yours?"

Two of the hounds then snarled at Crawford and charged him from two different directions. Colette was standing next to her father. One of the two hounds leapt at Shawn who raised his left hand and pointed it at the hound while it was in midair. A blue razor-like blue bolt of electric charge caught the animal in the chest and it exploded throwing pieces of bloody flesh everywhere.

Simultaneously, Colette side-stepped the other animal as it came for her head. As it sailed past the girl, it turned its head and came within inches of tearing off a portion of Colette's cheek. When it hit the ground behind her, he quickly turned and charged the girl's back. Colette half turned herself, now exposing the side of her body to the attacking hound while taking one step back. As the hound jumped, Colette quickly unsheathed a six-inch blade surrounded in a light blue light. The hound came abreast of the girl and she thrust the blade deep inside the underbelly of the animal. She held the weapon firmly and allowed the beast's momentum to continue moving forward while the blade did its work. The hound fell to the ground with an elongated cut line that slowly exposed the hound's inner organs. There was no further movement from the hound.

A sudden thunderclap broke the silence of the night and a circular light blue cloud descended and stopped over Sebago Lake. Its sides expanded in all directions like fog rolling in from the sea. It reached the remaining four wolfhounds and consumed them from sight. Within the thick blue mist, the hounds began crying out in insufferable pain. Then there was nothing but silence within.

The remaining witch appeared next to the demon in human form. She had blood all over the front of her robe. She hissed at Shawn and blood spewed forth from her red-stained teeth. Emily appeared to the right of Shawn and Colette and stood calmly beside her 12-year-old friend. The three stood resolutely before the vampire and witch. Shawn looked at both girls and nodded once.

"Ah, the girl finally shows herself," the vampire referring to Emily said. "Give me the Amulet girl and I will let you all live."

"You are weak, old man," Emily replied. "You will never have this symbol of Good. Your quest for evil dominance in this world ends here."

The demon and witch simultaneously charged the three before them. The witch flew at Emily who had raised the Amulet and stopped her charge completely as though the witch had hit an invisible wall. Colette approached the fallen woman and said, "You and your sisters will never attack or hurt another human being again. Have a wonderful time in hell!"

Colette quickly drew a circle representing Good around the semi-conscious witch. She stepped back and Emily bent down and touched the circle with her

Amulet. A fiery spark jumped off the Medallion and a circle of flames spread quickly around the still inert woman. The wall of fire grew to 10 feet in height. Within the wall of flame, the witch began shrieking in pain. This went on for 30 seconds, then silence. The fire extinguished itself and what remained in the circle was nothing a mound of ash.

Nearby, the vampire proceeded in Shawn's direction and raised his shiny ebony staff and pointed it directly toward Crawford's heart. Shawn raised both arms and extended them toward the oncoming demon.

Bolts of lightning-like energy, one red the other light blue, emanated from both adversaries. They collided half way between Crawford and the vampire created a loud thunderclap that was deafening. A succeeding bolt of red was shot at Shawn and he was hit in his left shoulder that turned him half way around. He gasped in pain and remained on his feet.

The vampire then closed in for the kill as both Colette and Emily stepped on either side of Crawford.

"I am going to annihilate you all!" shouted the vampire. As he raised his staff, he was hit from behind by a tremendous force. Cody had been let go from Sean's grasp and raced toward the black-cloaked figure. The vampire turned its head to face the aggressor and was met by a giant maw of very sharp teeth that bit into the old man's neck. Cody, holding the neck firmly, began shaking the head so violently that the main artery along with other blood vessels were severed completely. Cody then backed off when the dog noticed Emily step forward over the inert body. Fingers of the vampire began to twitch ever so slightly until their movement increased. The demon opened its fiery red eyes just as Emily shoved the Amulet into its mouth. She took a step rearward.

A red cloud-like mist rose from the vampire that was soon enveloped by a descending light blue vapor. The blue covered the red and several small lightning bolts were seen with the cloud mixture. Finally, they stopped and the vapors vanished completely leaving a mound of unrecognizable light blue soil showing.

Shawn had dropped to one knee while all this was occurring. When it was finally over, Colette stooped down beside her father and reached out to his injured shoulder. She put both of her hands on Shawn's seared flesh and closed her eyes. Crawford felt a healing warmth from her touch. 15 seconds later, the shoulder pain had stopped completely and he got to his feet.

Shawn looked at everyone as Sean Ross came over. Cody was sitting quietly beside Crawford. "Shawn, are you OK?" asked Ross.

"Yes, thanks to Emily and Colette. And I won't forget Cody. He probably saved us all, didn't you, boy?"

The German Shepherd reached up and licked Crawford's hand in appreciation.

With timing being everything, the Sheriff's Department Deputies began to arrive. Moments later, police cruisers from Gorham, Windham, and Standish pulled up to screeching stops. Officers exited their vehicles with weapons drawn. Ross stepped in front of his group and commanded everyone to stand down. It was all over. Gorham's Police Chief walked over and briefly spoke with Ross. He turned around and gave the same command to Officers around the vehicles. They holstered their weapons and walked slowly toward the Chief and the others.

Ambulances, four in total, arrived with sirens blazing. The Chief met with the drivers of each vehicle after they all exited their ambulances. They were instructed to slowly circumvent the Lake's shoreline to see if there were injuries or otherwise in the few occupied homes. A police cruiser was to lead the ambulances with a follow-on cruiser bringing up the rear. They were told to radio back to him on their progress around the Lake.

Sean and Shawn filled in the details of what had happened during the fight against the aggressors. The Chief, not being a pragmatist, was stunned at the news he was hearing. In his mind, there had to be a realistic reason for all of the noise that was heard miles away from the Lake. The Chief had come prepared to find more bodies, both human and animal. All he saw was a couple of dead animals that, like before, had been mutilated so much they were unrecognizable.

A call came in from the lead cruiser near the north end of the Lake. They had found two bodies, a man and a woman, whose necks had been nearly torn from their bodies. There were also some half dozen dogs that had been torn open around their neck areas. The Officer reporting gave the exact location and he and the ambulances, but one there on the scene of the report, continued their patrol toward the east end of Sebago Lake.

The Chief immediately sent two of his cruisers to the scene of the mutilations. The rear cruiser following the initial convoy of ambulances had remained behind to protect the two EMTs on site until the Chief's two cruisers arrived. As the two Police vehicles arrived, the one on stand-by roared off toward the initial convoy. One of the in-coming Police Officers found it odd that the Officer departing hadn't got out of his vehicle to brief them at the scene. He then focused on helping the ambulance drivers at their location. In seeing no one outside, the two Officers went up to the house and opened the front door. They were both met by the two EMTs from the parked ambulance. Both Officers and EMTs were never seen again.

EMILY

A Shawn Crawford Adventure

FOREWORD

Another challenge for me to write my second horror story. Using the same characters in my time travel novels, as well as the principal Character in my first horror rendition, Emily, I have attempted to 'connect the dots' in typing in these personalities so that the flow of the story will not be seen as awkward as the reader begins this narrative.

Shawn Crawford lends a character platform for Emily and Nathan Doerfler meeting in the desert wasteland outside the Gates of 12th Century Jerusalem during the height of the Third Crusades.

Nathan is the Holder of the Amulet that exudes extraordinary power in defending Good against Evil forces. Emily is the Instrument from which the Amulet demonstrates its power against all that attempts to deny everything that is decent worldwide.

This a very fast read and short narrative that will surely entertain. I hope that all will enjoy reading Emily as much as I did put it together.

Enjoy the Moment!

PROLOGUE

In the year 1197, the Third Crusades were at the forefront of the world's stage. The fight for the City of Jerusalem between the Crusaders and the Saracens was vicious and unending. Hundreds of soldiers died for the belief that there cause was a righteous one.

Shawn Crawford and his Cousin, Nate Doerfler, Physician's Assistant, were sent on a mission by their 2074 Australian Maritime Defense Base hierarchy to assess African Federation enemy movement in the Jakarta Islands. They had been caught up in a bluish cloud formation without warning. They exited the mist and found themselves in the 12th Century near the battle of the siege for Jerusalem. It was the Third Crusades.

After landing their advanced fighter aircraft, they were attacked by a small army of Crusader soldiers. Nathan was enlisted as a 'medical assistant' in their battle against the Saracens. Shawn was dragged to an outlying Christian camp not far from the Jerusalem gates.

Emily, a girl of twelve years of age, was sent to this time era from the 21st Century, more specifically the year 2017. She was an Agent of The Entity, a Galactic Force that protected the weak against those who would take advantage of their life's plight. She was sent to find the Amulet.

JERUSALEM

Emily walked among the bodies lying everywhere. Vultures had already descended. The plain of devastation was composed of hard-packed sand. Off in the distance, Emily saw the rooftops of Jerusalem, the Ancient City. Fires continued to burn within the City itself. There was no movement anywhere, save for the vultures. The year was 1198 A.D.

She continued to walk slowly among the dead and looked for one of the fallen in particular. The heat was searing with little wind to cool her. She expected to find the one individual in just a few minutes. Emily had been searching for 45 minutes. She had no description of the body, but she would know when she found him. After 10 more minutes of walking, she began to give up hope. There were so many, so many.

She passed a group of seven or eight who had fallen together. As she started to walk on, she saw a portion of a red arm band sticking out of a pile of three soldiers who had dropped to the ground simultaneously. The onslaught directed at these men must have been horrifying.

She stooped down beside the arm. Fingers twitched from nerve endings not yet put to rest. Emily moved one of the bodies aside and knew that she had found the one she was looking for. She reached into a jacket pocket and felt a warm glow in her hand. Emily withdrew the metallic object with a necklace fastened to it. It began to glow more brightly in her hands. The Amulet was what she had been searching for among all of the dead. Vultures began circling her and squawking wildly as if to warn that Emily's time was up among the dead. She moved aside as one of the birds settled down beside her brushing her shoulder on the way down to one of the bodies. The vulture looked back at her with blood red eyes. She didn't have long to wait.

A wall of black cloud began to materialize not far on the horizon. It grew in great proportion and seemingly advanced toward her with a purpose. She stood steadfast and faced the ominous wall of black approaching. Finally, the roiling mass of black mist came to a stop not six feet from where Emily stood. It did not then dissipate, but rather elevated itself into the air. What remained in its stead was a tall cloaked figure dressed all in black. He carried an ebony staff and stood before Emily while scrutinizing her with blood red eyes. He stood that way for several seconds without speaking.

Emily stood resolutely before him showing no emotion of fear. Finally, the man before her said, "Emily, Child. Give me the Amulet."

She continued to stare directly into his eyes and did not move. The figure bellowed in anger. "Give me the Amulet, Child, or I will destroy you right where you stand. This is your final warning. I will have that Amulet."

Emily moved forward a step and the Demon, for that was what it was, smiled ever so slightly. His eyes flickered a deeper reddish color. Instead of Emily's surrendering the glowing metallic piece, she raised it over her head. A bolt of bluish lightning shot from the Amulet and hit the Demon in the chest. It fell onto its back and howled in pain. Emily took another step forward and another bolt struck the fallen creature in the mid-section. Another howl of intense pain, and then silence as the black cloud formation descended and enveloped the inert Demon. When it dissipated, the Demon had vanished.

Emily fell to a knee and bent her head forward. She stayed in that position for several moments before lifting her head. Blood oozed from her nose as she struggled to get up off of the sand. A vulture hovered directly over her head, not less than 10 feet above. It dropped to the ground next to her feet and began squawking. The Amulet in her hand sent a blue lightning bolt through her closed fist directly into the bird's body. It disintegrated into ashes.

Emily picked herself up slowly and once erect, took several deep breaths. She then heard a soft moaning coming from the pile of soldiers behind her. Emily shuffled over to the dead bodies and saw an arm move upward. It was the man from whom she took the Amulet. Another moan from beneath one of the dead soldiers. With little strength left in her, she managed to move the top body away from the one pinned below.

He opened his eyes and said, "Emily?"

The girl knelt beside the man and placed the Amulet on his chest. This time, a transparent blue blanket covered the chest wound sustained during the recent battle. It rested over him for several moments. It then abruptly disappeared back into the Amulet.

Emily secured the Amulet and placed it within her white cloak. The man began to move and struggled to get to his feet. Emily took the man's arm and helped him get up. The exertion for her doing so caused her nose to begin dripping blood once again, She fell to her knees and then to the ground unconscious.

Emily awoke in a cave. She was lying on hard-packed sand and facing the outer entrance. It was night time. She noticed a figure standing very close to the entrance and looking outward. He wore a soldier's uniform and appeared very calm. The man looked behind him at Emily.

"You're awake. Good. How are you feeling, Emily?"

She couldn't quite make out his face but his tone of voice was very familiar. "Where am I and I think I know you, don't I?"

"Yes, Emily. I'm Nathan and you are a short distance from the battle site in a relatively small outcropping. I want to thank you for giving my life back to me."

"What happened to you, Nathan? I was searching for someone and driven to do so by a strong consciousness. When I found your body, I knew that it was you. And, more so, what you had in your possession. The Amulet."

"Yes, the Amulet. It has been my Protector for many years now. To answer your first question, I came from the year 2074. I left the Australian Continent with 'Sir' Shawn Crawford in a F-193B Leopard fighter aircraft. We were both assigned to the Maritime Air Defense Base there and had taken a flight to Jakarta. We were intercepted by The Entity who passed us through the time travel portal called the Gateway.

"Once cleared of all turbulence and the very thick bluish cloud, we found ourselves in the era of the Third Crusades. We could see the City of Jerusalem not far away. Shawn landed the Leopard behind a small hill mass and we exited the aircraft. No sooner had we had walked a dozen steps when we were set upon by a band of Christian soldiers on horseback.

"There were too many of them for us to escape their brutality. We were thought to be agents of the enemy Saracens. As they looked at our 'strange' metallic ship nearby, they thoroughly convinced themselves that we were demons. They tied us to their horses and we were nearly dragged to their camp a short distance from the Jerusalem walls.

"One of the soldiers had been struck by Shawn during our brief scuffle to escape. He could barely walk without pain. I convinced the leader that I had practiced the healing arts, the nomenclature of the era. The soldier's shoulder had fallen out of its socket and I applied just enough pressure to set it back in. It was then that the leader had confidence in me that I wasn't the demon he thought me to be. However, Shawn had lost consciousness while being dragged and he was put in chains at their camp site. I, on the other hand, was told to care for a couple of their wounded comrades.

"As I was successful in 'healing' their injured, I was tasked to ride with them to provide medical support during and following their battles with the Saracens. When you found me, I had been in the thick of a massive attack by the enemy who decimated every

EMILY

one of the Crusaders. I was not spared as I took a sword thrust into my chest. You found me sometime later. And now, about you. Please tell me why you are here looking for the Amulet."

"Nathan, I am here from the year 1748 and a small growing community in the State of Maine. I was orphaned when our Gorham Township settlement was attacked by Native Indians during the French and Indian War. My parents were both brutally killed and I was subsequently taken to a small fort on a hill to the East of the Town.

"A day later, a man from the Township, Samuel Bryant, was found semi-conscious not far from the fort's walls. I rushed to see if I could help him. When I got to him, he put his hand to my face and I felt a surge of something course through my body. It was not painful, but comforting.

"Since then, I had become an Agent of what I referred always to as The Entity. Strange that we know this Presence by the same name. Like you, I was sent on a "mission" to stop an evil Demon and his minions in the year 2017 from taking over the Town of Gorham. Its Mayor had been a shape-shifter. A resident who walked the Narragansett Trail in Town was a witch from the 18th century. An Indian that Bryant had killed during the war in the settlement re-surfaced from the dead. Together, the evil group met their demise at the hands of Shawn Crawford, a Doctor by the name of Wesolowski, and myself at the home of the O'Leary's within the Town.

"After the battle with evil, I remained in Gorham until one morning I awoke against a rock outcropping here in the Jerusalem area. I got up and felt a strong need to find one of the battle casualties and secure the Amulet he possessed in his shirt pocket. Once found, I was challenged for its possession by a Demon in black clothing and holding an ebony stick in his left hand.

The Amulet, not I, attacked the figure and drove it away. That is when I found you, Nathan."

KING SULTAN

A horseman suddenly appeared from around the corner of the cave entrance. He was dressed in white garments. His majestic horse was white in color with eyes the color of pale blue. He and the horse were surrounded by a pack of large dogs. There must have been 20 of them, all snarling and baring their teeth. Their eyes also shined with a light blue hue. A signal from the horseman instructed the pack to lie down on the sand. They obeyed and lay there staring up at their 'Master'.

The tall figure, regal in stature, dismounted and approached the cave entrance. Nathan and Emily had risen to their feet and stood waiting for something to happen. With his back to the pack of dogs, he raised his left arm in the air. There followed a swirling of the bluish dust around all of the dogs until they were all consumed by it. When it subsided to nothing, the animals had transformed into a group of men, all wearing white and kneeling behind their leader, waiting. "Rise," he said to the men behind him. They did as one.

The group looked to be seasoned soldiers, all fit and lightly armed with short-barreled automatic weapons. They looked like Uzis, but more modern in scope. They continued to stand with the weapons cradled in their arms.

'Who are you, Sir?" Emily asked. Nathan stood resolutely beside her and said nothing.

"My name is King Sultan. I was directed here by a Presence that more than insisted that I lead my men to this location. We have traveled far. Seeing the dead on the battlefield as we approached your location, I directed my men in the guise of wolfhounds to attack all vultures feeding on the dead remains.

Their work was more than efficient and now the dead lie in peace.

"I must ask you, young lady, as to the purpose of my being directed to your location. I sense that you are quite knowledgeable about these circumstances. What can you tell me?" "Your Highness," said Nathan, "With all due respect, we request your thoughtful consideration of what we are about to tell you. The young Lady, Emily, and myself were placed here from another time era. Yes, your Highness, I did say 'different', meaning that we traveled back in time to support the wishes of our Benefactor. Emily and I are from eras in the future." Nathan let that sink in for a moment. The King showed no emotion.

"I am from the year 2074 A.D. Emily is originally from the 18th Century, specifically 1748 A.D." Nathan continued to explain the events that eventually found them here. The King still showed no emotion.

Instead, he directed his men to begin setting up a camp nearby.

After explanations were given to the King, he turned around and walked over to one of the soldiers. He said something to him and the soldier bowed in respect and turned to his men. The second-in-command then issued orders to the group. Once again, he turned about and shape-shifted into a wolfhound. The 'animal' then began running toward the City of Jerusalem. The King turned and directed Emily and Nathan to sit with him on a regal carpet that had been placed in the sand nearby. Two of his soldiers stood nearby standing erect and ever watchful for any threat in the area.

"Your Highness," said Nathan, "The weapons your men carry appear to be from a modern era. Please forgive my being forward, how did they come by them?"

"Now it is time to tell our story, young Physician's Assistant. I am and all of my men are from the future as well, the year 2386. We come from a World State that was created as a result of what you refer to as the Fourth World War. Yes, I did say 'Fourth'. It occurred in the year 2213 A.D.

"The world as you know it had changed dramatically, not so much politically, but geographically as well. Our history taught us that the 21st Century was one of war, greed, and power-seekers. As if that wasn't enough for countries like the United States to have to deal with, the people suffered through environmental and weather-inducing events. The landscape changed significantly. Weather patterns became extreme. In the warm weather months, tornadoes struck everywhere. When rain fell, flood waters rose. In other parts of the country, drought was persistent, not only for a few months, but for a few years. Tens of thousands perished during these periods.

"During the cold weather months, no State was spared. The Northeast sustained unbearable cold weather and constant blizzard-like conditions day in and day out. Just to survive a day was a challenge for the Country had run out of heating fuel. Miami, Florida appeared to be hit the hardest because of the tremendous swings in temperature. For ten winters in a row, snow fell and temperatures dropped consistently to 30-degrees below zero. It seemed as though the world's poles had shifted.

"Again, tens of thousands died during these winter months. But the worst cataclysm were the earthquakes that started in California. The San Andrea's Fault split completely and the entire States of California, Oregon, and Washington were gone in a matter of minutes as they were all consumed and slid into a fiery crevice that measured 100 miles wide from the Canadian border to Baja California. The western shore became the State of Nevada.

Tens of millions were wiped out.

"The Rocky Mountains began spewing lava as volcanoes erupted taking more lives. Every country in the world suffered to varying degrees. It was as if God himself had pronounced the world as 'poisonous'. The African Countries were the least hit by cataclysmic devastation. Their governments took the opportunity to invade, not only Europe, but the Unites States as well. There was little military left to stop their advance.

"When the African coalition appeared to be in control of the world's countries that had suffered such significant catastrophe, a Western coalition had formed and began a counter-attack. This became known as the Fourth World War.

Every country in the world was affected.

"The use of atomic weapons was so prevalent that the earth's crust became affected. Small islands disappeared into the oceans. The United States was further topographically split on the East Coast as the damage rendered by constant atomic bombs took its toll. A line of demarcation saw the States of New York all the way to Alabama dropped drastically below sea level.

Tsunamis literally wiped out the East Coast.

"When the final bombs fell, a nuclear 'winter' existed. Survivors retreated underground and into deep caves. There, after decades of living in the dark, the atmosphere began to clear. They began to move out into the open. Small settlements began to form and farming was the only way to provide food.

Only the hearty survived. But it was enough to sustain life so the populations began to grow. But all of this took 125 years. Our land was but a shell of its former self. I now reign over an area the size of your State of Georgia. That is all that is left of your Country.

"Then close to 20 years ago, 'shadowy' figures began to appear everywhere. There were several 'types' that began to show themselves in settlements all over what was left of the world. Most people referred to them as 'Demons' for they appeared from nowhere. They wore black cloaks and they had eyes that were fiery red. Since then, when they appear with their minion shape-shifters, they have been unstoppable.

"They infect their victims with a touch of an ebony staff they all possess. Those 'touched' fall immediately to the ground and appear to have perished. Moments later, they rise and become shape-shifters and more minions for the Demons. Presently, there is a massive army of these creatures waiting to do the bidding of the controlling Demon.

"There is a Demon that appears to be above all others. From what you described to me once you found the Amulet, this was the Demon that you encountered, Emily. It is vicious, cunning, and vengeful. To stop all Demons and their armies, this is the one that must be annihilated. If this Demon falls, all others will cease to exist. Every one of them will turn to ash where they stand."

At that moment, a wolfhound appeared in their midst. It was bleeding from a shoulder wound. It walked slowly toward the King with staggered steps. As it fell to the ground, it changed shape into the soldier that had been dispatched to Jerusalem earlier. His wound was oozing blood. Nathan immediately looked at the King who nodded immediately. The Physician's Assistant went over to the soldier and knelt beside him. The soldier started to strike Nathan, but a sharp word from the King subdued the injured man. Nathan quickly evaluated the wound. A tip of an arrow was embedded in the shoulder's soft tissue. He reached into his pocket and extracted a small medical tools case. Nathan took a small pair of needle nose pliers out and began probing to acquire a secure hold on the fleshette. The soldier had to be in tremendous pain, but never showed it. He extracted the metal object.

Nathan asked if could have some water and two clean cloths. When that came, he flushed the wound and applied pressure to the wound with one of the cloths. Nathan took the second cloth and applied it around the initial cloth and secured it with a knot. The soldier still in pain grabbed Nathan's forearm and squeezed it. While doing so, he smiled at the young PA. His body took over and he fell asleep.

The King came over and knelt beside Nathan. He looked at the young man for several seconds. As he got up, he pressed his left hand on Nathan's left shoulder as a measure of gratitude to what the PA had done.

"Jerome is one of my best Soldiers. He would have been sorely missed had you not taken the action you did. Well done, Nathan.

"Now everyone," he addressed his men, "Rest, for tomorrow we fight the Demon and his minions for the final time. And Emily and Nathan, that is when we will free your Pilot Shawn Crawford. Now, please sleep for the morning will be upon us shortly."

SHAWN CRAWFORD

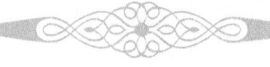

Shawn had hit his head several times while being dragged by the Saracen Horseman. He finally passed out. When he awoke after midnight, he was trussed up in chains and lying on his back. As his vision cleared, he took note of every detail of his surroundings. A tether line was just above his head. It kept the horses from roaming around a small oasis. One of the animals seemed to take a liking to Crawford as it kept hitting its face against the back of Shawn's head. Wish I had an apple, he thought.

A couple of hours later, he opened his eyes for a moment and saw a huge wolfhound with pale blue eyes not six inches from his face. Shawn did not panic, but felt a sense of calm and relief. The animal sniffed Crawford's clothing and looked again into the captive's eyes. He backed away and bowed at the same time.

A shout rang out in the camp and arrows began landing in the area of the retreating wolfhound. It took one in the shoulder and went down to the sand for a brief moment. The huge dog immediately got up and began running out of the camp. He sides swiped a pole holding the tethered line for the horses causing the majority of the arrow's shaft to break off. It escaped without further injury and into the desert night.

Shawn watched the Crusader fighters scatter around the camp in anticipation of more 'wild' animals coming within the periphery of their station. No others appeared and after 10 minutes their leader told all to stand down. A few additional guards were selected to walk outside the perimeter to provide defense and early warning. The leader checked on Shawn who feigned sleep. He kicked Crawford in the leg to make certain that the hound had not killed him. Shawn answered with a slow moan. Satisfied that their captive was alive and secured, the leader went back to his tent to get some sleep.

Back at the cavern, King Sultan aroused his troops. Jerome was feeling better as they all had their meager meals. The King was in the middle of them and began talking about their next mission. Jerome told the King about the layout of the Saracen camp. He also recognized weak points in their defense and shared these with the others.

King Sultan then had Jerome stick-outline the camp and what sentries there were when he had arrived at the enemy's location. Everything was drawn in detail. The King then devised his plan of action by assigning each soldier a specific point of entry. The goal was to free Shawn Crawford from captivity before the Christians had an opportunity to take him within the

Jerusalem gates. If that happened, the success of their mission would deteriorate significantly.

Questions were asked of both Jerome and King. They were answered with tactical operation in mind. This was going to be a 'snatch and grab' mission with immediately retrieval to a rally point the King noted on the map in the sand. There were two and a half hours before sun would rise. The group prepared for their assault.

Nathan and Emily were told to remain where they were in the King's absence. They would soon be sent after to join the group at a different and safe location. Nathan approached the King and offered the Amulet for additional protection. Soltan took it and the metallic object began to glow a pale blue color. It was warm to his touch even beneath the gloves he was wearing. He thanked Nathan and told them to wait until a member of his until returned to take them to the other location.

The King saluted Both Nathan and Emily, turned his white steed, and ordered his men to transition.

Every soldier knelt and assumed the appearance of a huge wolfhound. They split into four groups of five and began running toward the enemy's camp with Jerome in the lead. The King galloped after them.

Four of the King's 'men' went ahead of the rest and acted as 'scouts'. Under the darkness of the night, they positioned themselves at the key points of entry into the Christian camp. King Sultan halted his white steed some 50 meters away and behind a small hillock. Two of the scouts took our Saracens who were providing perimeter defense. They had transitioned back to human form and shot the enemy combatants in the back of the heads. Their modern automatic weapons had a unique suppressor and silencer built into the end of the barrel. Not a sound was heard as the men dropped dead to the sand.

All of the point men and scouts then turned in the direction of the King's location. Each soldier took a mini flash light and individually sent a signal. Soltan then sent his remaining force into the camp where they transitioned into human form. As the sentries had been eliminated, the remaining Saracens were caught sleeping. Each one was shot once in the head where they lay.

Shawn was watching the entire operation. Jerome came over to him in human form, bent down, and freed Crawford from his chains. As he got to his feet, he felt dizzy and started to sway to one side. Jerome immediately picked up Shawn and shoulder-carried him to a safe distance away from the fire zone. It was then that the King came galloping over.

Shawn struggled to his feet as Soltan dismounted. The latter came over, stopped in front of him, and watched him for several seconds. Crawford kept shaking his head as if to clear the 'cobwebs'. When his vision returned, he found King Sultan kneeling and bowing in front of him. Crawford was at a loss as to what to or say and waited for the King to rise.

"Shawn Crawford, we have been waiting for you. I must admit that it took the Entity a while to send you to us. Typical of His Blueness," as he raised his eyes to the heavens.

"Sir, I must apologize, but do I know you?"

As the King began to explain what was going on, one of his wolfhounds came running up to him, knelt, and transformed into human shape. He appeared agitated and out of breath, for a wolfhound.

"Speak, Kotor," the King demanded.

"Your Highness," Kotor began, "The Demon and his minions are approaching. They will soon arrive at the girl's location. Your Highness, if we are to save them, we must hurry." Kotor backed away still bowing as the King called all of his soldiers to his immediate area. They knelt before their King. Shawn watched in amazement as all transformed into huge wolfhounds.

"'Sir' Shawn, please take one of the Saracen's stallions and ride with me. Emily and Nathan are in immediate danger. We must hurry if we are to protect them."

Shawn thought, Nathan? My cousin is still alive? And what is Emily doing here from the 21st Century and the Gorham Township. No time for answers to be given. He jumped upon a jet-black stallion and galloped after King Sultan on his white steed. He caught up and trailed behind and to his left.

Soltan urged him to ride abreast.

"Your Friends were found after a devastating battle not far from Jerusalem. Your Cousin, I'm told, and don't ask by whom, was enlisted in the Crusaders' Army as a 'Medic'. He nearly perished in the Saracen enemy assault and was found by Emily. She took the Amulet from Nathan and drove the High Demon away as it tried to force it from the girl. And now, it has returned with his reinforcements to finish what he had set out to do."

'Jerome', the Wolfhound, raced in front of the King and led him to the shortest distance to intercept the Demon and its army of 'zombies' from Emily and Nathan's location. They arrived minutes before the ominous black swirling cloud arrived. In the background, a horrific noise of advancing death-like figures was heard and approaching rapidly.

Twenty meters from where Emily and Nate stood in awe of the advancing cloud, King Sultan and his small 'army' stopped beyond them and acted as a miniature shield. Shawn had peeled off behind the King and came to Emily and Nathan.

"Shawn, are you alright?" Nathan asked. "Not to worry Cousin, but I am a bit hungry. Do you have some snacks on you?" Nate just rolled his eyes.

"I'm glad to see that you are alright yourself. And, Emily, what a pleasant surprise! Haven't seen you in 'ages'," quipped Shawn. Emily too rolled her eyes.

The swirling black mass stopped 30 meters in front of Soltan and his Hounds. The black-cloaked then figure appeared as the mass of ether rose sharply above him and remained in stasis. The Demon stared at those before him with a wide smile on his face. Again, its eyes were blood red in color.

"Soltan, Soltan, I am not surprised to find you here." Two of the zombies then raced in front of the Demon with the intent to attack the human forms before them. Two of the Wolfhounds leapt forward and intercepted them. The 'undead' were torn to pieces. The Hounds then retreated back to their 'pack'.

The Demon raised his staff and forcefully pushed it into the sand beside him. His minions cowered in fear and no longer approached. Meanwhile, King Sultan's Wolfhounds all knelt in front of their King and transformed into human figures, all heavily armed with their modern automatic weapons.

"Soltan," the Demon stated, "Is this all necessary, the armed 'armada' you have with you. You must be joking. Let's cut to the 'chase', as if there will be one," he smirked. "Hand the Amulet over to me and we will quietly withdraw. This is all I want. No big decision if you want to be spared."

Sultan's Army then retracted their rifle charging handles thereby loading a bullet into their chambers and stood prepared for the attack. The King just smiled and indicated that the day had just begun and why not have a little fun. It was then that Emily walked up slowly and stood beside the King. The Amulet was in her right hand.

EMILY

"As you wish and yours will be death to all." The Demon raised its staff and pointed it in the direction of the small knot of men and Emily. The zombies rushed forward.

Emily raised the Amulet skyward and a strong blue lightning bolt arced skyward. As it fell to the ground it created a pale blue mist that blanketed the thousands of approaching zombies. As it descended, the Demon yelled out, "No!!"

The bluish cloud reached the ground not more than five feet in front of Soltan's Army. Time stopped. After a full minute's time, it began to dissipate. When it was gone, nothing remained of the Demon's zombies. The Demon itself lay on the ground withering in pain. As it tried to get up, Emily approached and pointed the Amulet directly at the Demon's head. Another bolt of lightning struck forward and hit the face full force causing the head to explode. The remainder of the bodily form rose from the ground in ashes and the black swirling cloud descended over it. Once covered, the Demon and its cloud mass disappeared.

The King dismounted and went over to Emily. He stood beside her for a brief moment before speaking.

"Emily, what you have done is cleanse the world of a vicious evil, like that of a plague, that would have devoured everyone on this planet. Your bravery has not gone unnoticed by my men."

Emily turned and saw that they all had knelt before her with heads bowed. She asked that they all rise. Standing before them, she told the soldiers that their bravery was second to none. And that their Leader, the King, was a monumental figure that all should be proud of serving. She then turned to Shawn and Nathan.

"We will meet again. This world of ours, regardless of the time era, is never safe from the evil that walks the earth. You will always be my Guardians."

Emily was then enveloped by the pale blue mist and disappeared from view. All were quiet.

"Shawn, 'Sir' Shawn, I should say, our Benefactor in blue never ceases to amaze. I wish you and your young Medical Assistant safe travels."

King Sultan then signaled to his soldiers and they immediately transformed into Wolfhounds. Soltan waved good-bye, turned, and he the pack galloped off to the west. They were soon gone from sight.

Shawn then looked at Nathan and said, "looks like we have a way to walk, unless we can get this Saracen black stallion to carry us both." The horse shook its head up and down.

They rode for several miles and found their F-193B Leopard Fighter exactly as they left it. Around the aircraft, there were mounds of ash. Shawn, in noting this, raised an eyebrow and scanned the landscape before him.

Without saying another word, they both climbed into the Leopard and prepared for takeoff.

As the engines spooled up, a swirling black cloud approached the fighter from the rear and 'oozed' its way into the rear fuselage compartment. Shawn seeing that all panel indicators were in the 'green', rotated the Leopard and the aircraft rose sharply into the sky.

They were soon met by The Entity's pale blue cloud mass and came out the other side nearing the Australian Maritime Defense Base.

They never heard the hollow laughter coming from the rear compartment until it was too late.

KENNEBUNK

FOREWORD

The conclusion to the book Emily: A Horror Story saw Shawn Crawford, Nathan Doerfler, and the 12-year-old Girl leaving the 12th Century and the outskirts of Jerusalem in their hypersonic advanced jet fighter, the F-193B Leopard. They had narrowly escaped from a harrowing experience dealing with Crusaders and Saracens who battled one another for control of the Holy City. The three had been caught in the middle. A specter, a Demon, coveted an ancient copper-like Medallion that had been previously secured by Nathan and Emily. As Shawn directed Nathan and Emily to get aboard the stealth fighter, they were unknowingly pursued by the Demon who managed to steal itself away in the back cargo compartment of the aircraft. Shawn was able to launch the Leopard and leave the 12th. Century behind enroute to the Sydney Australian Maritime Base in the year 2074 through a time travel gateway.

When they exited the fighter at the Airbase, each felt a sigh of relief for having escaped the evil that had sought to kill them. Or, was it really an escape or a demonic transference from one ancient time to that of a modern era?

CAST OF CHARACTERS

FIRST LIEUTENANT WILL CARUSO: Royal Australian Plane Captain to the F-42A Tiger Shark and B-193B Advanced Fighter Aircraft. Highly intelligent, irreverent and carefree spirit and Crew Chief with a meticulous eye problem solving with regard to all Fixed-Wing and Rotary-Wing Aircraft in the Defense platform inventory. Awarded the Meritorious Service Medal for his accomplishments in the area of aircraft fighter support to the Royal Australian Air Force. Member of The Entity's Inner Circle. Time era origination: 2074.

SERGEANT MADELYN COFFILL: Royal Australian Air Force, Chief Administrative Assistant 'Gatekeeper' for Marshal Allison Morrison. Very efficient in the performance of her duties while displaying an intemperate exterior, but harboring a heart of gold and boundless inner kindness. Chief Guardian to Colette Roberts-Crawford in the absence of Lady Christine Roberts. Time era origination: 2074.

SIR STEVEN SHAWN CRAWFORD: Air Marshal, Royal Australian Air Force, former Lieutenant Colonel, United States Army, Husband to Lady Christine Roberts, Father to Christopher and Colette, Pilot, OH-58D Kiowa Warrior, AH-1G Cobra Gunship and RAH-66 Comanche Attack Helicopters. The F-42A Tiger Shark and F-193B Leopard Advanced Stealth Fighter Aircraft. Moral, modest, and irreverent contributor to every major of personnel involvement. Chief expert in the understanding of Gateway/Wormhole events. Principal deterrent to the assassination attempts on the lives of various historical figures. Audacious and fierce devotee toward protecting the rights of those oppressed. Twice awarded the United States Medal of Honor, a Hero in the Third World War, Seventh Degree Black Belt Martial Arts Specialist and Expert in the art of Silent Killing. Speaks eight foreign languages and former Delta Force Black Ops Member. Triple Ace against enemy Air Force Aggressors in aerial combat. Holds a Doctorate Degree in Advanced Aeronautical Engineering and Quantum Mechanics with Degrees in Economics and Chemistry from Georgia Southern University. Member of the Australian Government's Intelligence Agency. Never misses a good Beef Wellington dinner. Favorite of The Entity. Time era origination: 2017.

CHRISTINE ROBERTS-CRAWFORD: The temporal Mother of Christopher and Colette Roberts-Crawford. Wife of Shawn Crawford. F-22 Raptor Pilot who recorded more than 15 aerial 'kills' while flying against German Nazi Aircraft during a time travel sojourn. Given the Title of 'Lady' Christine for her role in saving the Australian Ambassador in the year 2074. Proficient in flying both the F-42A Tiger Shark as well as the F-193B Leopard Advanced Stealth Fighter Aircraft. An Agent of The Entity. Time era origination: 2017.

CHRISTOPHER ROBERTS-CRAWFORD: The temporal Son of Shawn and Christine. Seventh Degree Black Belt Martial Arts Specialist. Speaks eight foreign languages. An advanced Fighter Pilot with more than 10 aerials 'kills' making him a Double Ace. Speaks at World Symposiums relating to his knowledge of time travel, quantum physics and the Universe. Is 16 years of age. An Agent and Son of The Entity. Time era origination: Always.

COLETTE ROBERTS-CRAWFORD: The temporal Daughter of Shawn and Christine. Loves to tweak her Father's nose when the latter is mischievous. Has the power to bring individuals back from the dead. An Advanced Fighter Pilot at the age of 10 years old. Precocious, loving and caring for those in need. An Agent and Daughter of The Entity. Time era origination: Always.

JOLIE O'LEARY-CRAWFORD: Cousin to Sir Shawn Crawford through her marriage to Thomas Crawford. Heir to a billion-dollar inheritance following the sudden death of her Husband Thomas. Time era origination: 2017.

EMILY: A perpetual 12-year-old Girl who has the ability to conquer Evil through the use of a Medallion with an ancient script. Defeated the Demon along the Narragansett Trail in Gorham, Maine with Sir Shawn Crawford and Tim O'Leary. Overcame another Demon during the late 12th Century during the Third Crusades. An Agent of The Entity. Time era origination: Always.

NATHAN DOERFLER: Physician's Assistant who was brought back to life several times by The Entity. Seventh Degree Black Belt in the Martial Arts. An

Agent of The Entity who has traveled through time on numerous occasions to fulfill missions give to him by The Entity. Holds two Doctoral Degrees from Georgia Southern University in Medical Science and Physics. Cousin to Sir Shawn Crawford. Personally, stopped the assassination of President John F. Kennedy in Dallas, Texas in November 1963. Time era origination: 2017.

ROBERTO 'BOB' JESUS GONZALES: OH-58D Pilot from the 341st Aviation Helicopter Group, amicably referred to as 'The Chief'. Unit Historian and renowned Helicopter Pilot commanding respect for his exception helicopter flying skills. Awarded the Distinguished Service Cross and Silver Star for aerial performance of duty beyond all expectations against opposing enemy forces. Principal Paternal Influence and Mentor to the totally irreverent Shawn Crawford. Back-seat Radar Intercept Officer in the F-22B Raptor during anti-drug related missions in South America. Presently serves the Australian Sydney Air Defense

Force as the Air Commodore, Pilot of the F-42A Tiger Shark Stealth Fighter, RAH-66 Comanche and AH-1G Cobra Attack Helicopters. Chief Rotary-Wing Instructor for the Australian Sydney Air Defense Force.

ADMIRAL J. HUNTER KING: Charismatic Special Operations [SEAL/Delta Force] Leader fluent in seven languages specializing in Arabic and Swahili. Seventh Degree Black Belt in the Art of Silent Killing. Holds a dual Doctorate Degree from American University in International Studies and from the Massachusetts Institute of Technology (M.I.T.) in Advanced Fusion Quantum Mechanics. Built his first mini-jet fighter at the age of 11. Married to equally charismatic Kathleen. Veteran of the African Wars. Time era origination: 2017.

DONALD LAGACE: CIA Operative and Time Traveler, Agent for The Entity, Principal Organizer in the operation causing abrupt cessation of the Third

World War hostilities in 2018. Part-time Musician and Contributor to famous Scores such as The Star-Spangled Banner. Time era origination: Always.

MARSHAL ALLISON MORRISON: Senior Officer commanding the Australian Sydney Air Defense Base. Wife of Air Chief Marshal Michael O'Leary. Outstanding and charismatic Leader of all aerial forces on the Continent of Australia. Directed victory against the incursion of African Federation Forces into Australia. Time era origination: 2074.

AIR CHIEF MARSHAL MICHAEL O'LEARY: Royal Australian Air Force, former Lieutenant Colonel, United States Air Force, Husband to Marshal Allison Marshall. F-42A Tiger Shark Stealth Fighter Pilot and Mentor to Sir Shawn Crawford. Gained Fighter Pilot Ace status when he traveled back in time to conduct aerial battles against aggressors during World War II and the Korean War. Wounded in action. Time era origination: 2053.

SANCHA: The Automated Voice Recognition System aboard the newest Attack Stealth Fighter Aircraft, the F-98A Stingray. Responds only to voice recognition commands given by Sir Shawn Crawford.

THE ENTITY: An Intergalactic Being who is the Champion of Good over Evil. Employs Agents to traverse through a Gateway that enables them to go back into the past and deny assassination attempts on lives of influential individuals who serve only what is Good and Righteous in their own time eras. Utilizes Sir Shawn Crawford as His principal Agent to correct world injustices. Time era origination: Always.

PROLOGUE

The screams were excruciating to hear, if there was anyone around to notice at 11:30 pm. Footsteps steeped in blood led to the upstairs second story of this magnificent three-tiered mansion located in an affluent section of Kennebunk, Maine. A young woman drenched in her own blood was in a spacious bedroom near a night stand. She crawled closer to the ornate piece of furniture. The woman reached upward toward the phone that was lying now only inches away above her. As her bloodied hand grasped the receiver to pull it to her, her attacker bent quickly at the waist and bit into the woman's exposed neck. There was no scream of pain, but merely a whimper, almost of delight. The phone fell on the carpet beside her. The 'man' then propped her up against the nightstand and drove a sharp serrated blade into her back pinning her temporarily to the drawer of the stand. Blood gurgled from her mouth as she very slowly slumped to the floor beside her huge king-sized bed. Her eyes were wide in shock and then a milky film covered them as she drew her final breath.

Her attacker, looking down at her, said, "I will await your return shortly. You belong to me, now, and will forever to serve me for a higher purpose." Then, he was gone.

SEVEN HOURS LATER

Police cruisers circled the expansive driveway while detectives surveyed the second-floor area. The State Police Crime Unit was in the process of taking samples and photographing anything and everything that had a blood stain on it. Meanwhile, the maid who had arrived by 6:45 AM was still in hysterics. A woman police officer was sitting with her and trying to get her to calm down after seeing the body upstairs. This was going to take a long while.

The Medical Examiner was in the process of making a preliminary evaluation of the condition of the body before it was taken downstairs and into a waiting ambulance. Police at the main gate had their hands full with keeping spectators and drivers moving along the very narrow two-lane road off the grounds.

The house was considered old by present standards, but had been completely re-furbished as soon as the deceased had move into it five years prior. The view from the inside living room was breath taking. Ocean waves were seen crashing heavily on the rocks below, The wrap around decking afforded a 180-degree view of the Atlantic Ocean. Those present at this moment had only an imaginative thought as to how gorgeous the sunrise must have been every morning during this incredible summer weather. Many in the local area considered it a mansion in every regard.

As detectives canvassed the area for any evidence that might lend a clue as to the killer or any motive involved, a young man with sandy-colored hair approached the ambulance and spoke with the

Medical Examiner briefly. The M.E. was seen raising his hands in a submissive nature while the newcomer entered the back of the vehicle and secured the door from the inside.

The lead detective, who had arrived soon after the maid called the incident in, came out the front door and walked over to the ambulance. The Medical Examiner was animatedly talking to the driver of the vehicle and explaining what had just happened. The detective asked what the commotion was all about and the M.E. told him that a young man had approached him and told him that 'he' now had jurisdiction of the case and wanted to see the body.

The officer said something expletive deleted and proceeded to the back door. He opened it abruptly. What the detective saw inside simply amazed him. There was no one inside the vehicle. The detective turned to the M.E. and driver and asked them if this was some kind a joke! If it was, where was the body? The Examiner quickly looked inside himself and stared in disbelief at finding no one there.

The detective then called his personnel together and gave orders to inspect the grounds for anything that might lead to the disappearance and discovery of a body that simply 'walked off' without an explanation. Nearly an hour went by and the body remained undiscovered. In the interim, communication was sent to local law enforcement officials in Kennebunkport, Ogunquit, Wells, Dayton, and Biddeford, along with a sketchy description of the individual who had entered the rear of the ambulance. By nightfall, no positive information surfaced. Law enforcement personnel were simply baffled, even more so with the negative reports coming in from the Maine State Police and their efforts along the Maine Turnpike, both North and South.

The victim had been identified as one Jolie O'Leary Crawford. She was in her mid-30's and was recently widowed. Her late Husband Thomas Crawford had made his fortune in oil, specifically from creating rigs in the Gulf of Mexico that were engineered to withstand more than 185-mile per hour sustainable winds. The engineering feat he devised was nothing short of genius. His models soon were replicated in the most hazardous regions of the world, more notably in the ever-changing vicious weather of the North Sea.

Thomas traveled frequently due to his ownership of oil companies around the world. His vision was that of ultimate safety for all of his off-shore personnel in the production and retrieval of oil worldwide. He had devoted more than four years of his time studying and evaluating rig construction all over the world. Eighteen months earlier than the scene of the vicious murder of his Wife in Kennebunk, Thomas was attending a dinner in his honor in Bahrain for his foresight and ingenuity in setting new safety standards for oil rig construction. As he was concluding his speech before a large audience representing European and African consortium's, he passed out at the lectern and fell to the dais. Medical examiners later ascertained that he had suffered an aortic rupture. His death had been immediate.

Jolie had been devastated to learn of her Husband's passing. They had been romantically close through their 11 years of matrimony. No children resulted from their relatively brief marriage. The insurance settlement was astronomical. Jolie had been taken care of for the remainder of her life.

In the previous three months, she had been taken by the charm of an affluent Austrian who had recently moved overseas from Salzburg. His name was Igor Tarzanian. He had gained his wealth from mortuary granite stone design inventiveness for the relatives of the rich and famous European nobility.

Tarzanian's unique ability to capture the essence of the deceased in granite stone was renown. The elite in several European countries had already commissioned his future work to be personally displayed as tombstones for years to come following their deaths and internment.

Tarzanian and O'Leary-Crawford had met at an exclusive art exhibit in Portland. The Artist Salvador Dali's paintings renown worldwide was presented for viewing one evening only for New England's elite. *Swans Representing Elephants*, reputed to be Dali's second-most famous painting, had been advertised to be exhibited. It was coincidence that Mr. Tarzanian and Ms. O'Leary-Crawford had remained together at the site of the painting after others had moved on. Following small talk about the work before them, the Austrian invited her to join him for a drink at the Hampton where he was staying. Mr. Tarzanian was now a person of interest. And, curiously had suddenly disappeared.

THE DECEASED

The young sandy-colored hair 'intruder' into the back of the ambulance at the Kennebunk murder scene was a Joseph Shawn Crawford. He was from the future, specifically the year 2074. His pedigree was considered normal middle class. Shawn's accomplishments, however, were yet another remarkable side of him. He held two Doctorate Degrees from Georgia Southern University in Statesboro, Georgia. Crawford had no discerning issues with problematic equations dealing with Quantum Physics or Advanced Chemistry. He also was fluent in seven different languages.

Shawn was viewed as a likable and docile individual until an injustice against the weak in the world was thrust in his direction. Crawford had a seventh Degree Black Belt in the Martial Arts, notably the Wing Tsun defensive style of self-defense. He had no patience with lack of manners, civility, or common decency.

His employment background was a prolific example of what a true military warrior exemplified. His service included graduating from the Army's premier flight program at Fort Rucker, Alabama. There, he earned his wings as a Warrant Officer One and quickly transitioned from Black Hawk to Cobra Gunship Helicopters. Before being assigned to his regular Unit, Shawn was approached by the Central Intelligence Agency who believed his language skills would prove beneficial to the Country's fight against the ever-mounting terrorist threat against the United States and its Allies. His service through the CIA was impressive, so much so that, as very few of those before him, he was awarded the Agency's highest Medal of Honor. An award, of course, that he was never able to display on any uniform either in the military or in the civilian sector. As he completed his final clandestine mission in Syria where he took out the number one ISIS fighter by sending him to the virtual and endless awaiting virgins in heaven, he was assigned to a South American Unit to fly OH-58D Kiowa Helicopters. The operation there was to curb the constant flow of drug cartel inflow shipments to the United States via Central America and Mexico. It was then that he had had his first-time travel event experience.

His rise to 'stardom' had been meteoric. Shawn Crawford was an Agent of The Entity, an Intergalactic Being who protected all who were 'Good' versus the forces of 'Evil' in the world, in any time era. He had saved Presidents of the United States and other very important Dignitaries from assassinations.

The Australian Government had bestowed upon him the honor of 'Knighthood' for his bravery and commitment to peace in the face of tremendous peril of all who would do harm to all within the Continent.

Crawford's exploits since then were legendary. His presence at the home of the dead woman was not incidental and served a purpose, a personal one at that. Jolie O'Leary-Crawford had been Shawn's Cousin via her marriage to Thomas. Shawn, Thomas and Jolie had grown up together in the same neighborhood complex and were close during their childhood years. She and Thomas were two years older than Shawn. Jolie and Shawn early on seemingly had a way of 'connecting' with one another, almost as though one knew what the other person was thinking. They were precocious and on the same page with core values that typified an awareness of what was decent in the world.

Jolie had awakened with a start in the rear of the ambulance. Shawn sat on the opposite side of the vehicle and smiled down at her. She was wide-eyed at first and started hyper-ventilating. Crawford reached over and placed his hand on Jolie's shoulder and said, "Easy, Coz. You're safe now."

She started to get up while noticing the blood-stained sheet that covered her body. "What's happening? Shawn? What are you doing here? And why am I in what looks like a medical vehicle?"

"Jolie, we don't have much time," he said as she stared back at him with total disbelief at her present status. "I will tell you everything once we are away from here, OK?"

Shawn grabbed Jolie's right hand. Immediately, they were surrounded by a light blue haze that consumed the rear of the ambulance. There was a sudden 'bump' against the back of the vehicle and the rear door cracked open. A shallow breeze entered the ambulance, albeit for a millisecond. In a matter of seconds, they found themselves in a highly advanced fighter aircraft. He was in the left seat of the jet fighter. In the right seat, was another pilot whom she had never seen before. She looked over to her left and saw a young girl watching her intently from her seat beside her.

"Hello, Jolie, my name is Emily and welcome aboard the F-193B Leopard Stealth Fighter piloted by no other than your Cousin Shawn. In the seat in front of you is a young and charming Physicians' Assistant, now turned Fighter Pilot, by the name of Nathan Doerfler." The latter raised his glove hand and waved back to Jolie.

"Shawn, shall I fill in this very bewildered relative of yours, or would you like to take the honor of doing so?" Emily asked.

"Emily, please inform my dear Cousin as to where we are, where we're going, and why she is gracing us with her company." Nate looked over at his Mentor with a side-long glance and smirked. Crawford then leaned back against the head-rest and closed his eyes. "Nathan, please let me know when we are in the Sydney Control Zone. You have the aircraft, Mr. Doerfler."

"I have the aircraft, Boss." Shawn turned his head slightly to the right, opened his right eye to look at his Protegee, smiled, and fell fast asleep. Emily then asked Nate if he had ever flown before they met in the Jerusalem Desert in the year 1198. Doerfler politely answered in the negative, although he said that did feel very high during one night at the Officers' Club at the Fort Sam Houston Army School of Medicine while finishing up his course work.

Jolie, still suffering from the trauma from the previous evening, turned toward Emily who attempted to allay the Former's anxiety by offering an explanation as to what was happening. "Jolie, what was the very last thing you remembered?"

"I was in my home with Igor Tarzanian. We had just attended a Play at the Ogunquit Play House and were settling in to enjoy the remainder of the evening. I told him that I was going upstairs to freshen up when he suddenly grabbed me from behind. He had a horrific look to him. His eyes were a deep crimson and he smiled as he pulled me toward him. I told him that he was hurting me, but he persisted. At this point, I was terrified. I reached to the side and picked up a heavy brass statue of Diana from an end table and swung it hitting him on the side of his head. As he let me go, I raced for the stairs and to my bedroom to lock the door. But he was unbelievably fast in recovering from the blow. I nearly got the bedroom door closed behind me when he literally crashed into the room and knocked me on my back. Igor then placed his hand to the side of my head and he proceeded to bite down on my neck. He raised his head with two fang-like teeth dripping with blood. I started to turn to reach for the bedside phone, but I felt this horrible knife-like sensation in my back. After that, nothing but blackness. Then, I saw Shawn sitting beside me in the back of the ambulance. Everything afterward was a blur, until now."

Emily reached over and grabbed her hand. "You're safe now, Jolie. We are taking you to the year 2074 and to Sydney, Australia. You will be safe there. In a matter of moments, we will be traversing through a 'gateway' that will allow the aircraft to 'jump forward' in time. Later, after we land in Sydney and you've had the opportunity to recuperate from your ordeal, we will offer an explanation as to how this can be achieved. Suffice it to say, this is not Shawn Crawford's 'first rodeo' in experiencing time travel. As a matter of fact, all three of us have managed have gone through this time portal on a number of occasions."

"Shawn," Nathan said, "We are about to make the transition. The light bluish cloud at your eleven o'clock."

"OK, Nate. I've got the aircraft. Jolie and Emily, there will be some slight turbulence as we enter the cloud mass. No need to be worried. Here we go."

The Leopard shook, but not uncontrollably. They were out of the bluish cloud in a matter of seconds. On the horizon, and over an azure body of water, was a land mass. Shawn made a radio call and was immediately answered by an aircraft controller. The latter directed him into a landing pattern and they were soon on the tarmac at the Sydney Australian Maritime Defense Base in the year 2074. Crawford taxied the airplane into a huge hangar where he spooled down the engines. They exited the aircraft after they were met by two aircraft maintenance personnel who had immediately chalked the airplane and assisted both Jolie and Emily out of the Fighter.

THE SYDNEY CRISIS

As they were departing the huge aircraft shelter, the Base Commander Marshall Allison Morrison's vehicle approached and stopped in front of them. Morrison was a charismatic Leader of Australia's chief defensive aerial system that had fought successfully against African Federation intruders on the northern shores of the Continent. She was highly regarded by the Australian Government's leadership and her wisdom to guide had never been in question.

They proceeded over to Morrison's Office where they were met by top officials in the Australian Air

Defense Base Operations. Air Chief Marshall Michael O'Leary, Morrison's Husband, Bob Gonzales, Christine Roberts, Shawn's Wife, and Christopher, Shawn's Son, all rose from their seats when Morrison and company entered. Madelyn Coffill, Morrison's Gatekeeper, took orders for coffee and lattes from the group. They all sat down comfortably in the Commander's spacious office.

Shawn proceeded to brief everyone regarding their transition from Kennebunk, Maine 2017 to present day. Jolie sat beside Emily and looked down at the carpet. The latter noted her anxiety and grabbed her hand in hers. This was not lost on Crawford as he finished his briefing to those present.

'Jolie and Emily, you will be staying with Michael and me this evening. You will be safe there and will be afforded the opportunity to 'decompress' from your recent experience," Morrison said. "Shawn, I need to talk to you about events just now occurring in Sydney after we break from this meeting." Coffill knocked softly and she and another airman carried the beverages into the room. After everyone had his/hers, Morrison asked Doerfler if he had anything to add. Nate replied in the negative. The Commander then looked at Emily who declined comment for the moment. She looked over at Shawn who had an eyebrow raised at her reply.

After 10 minutes, the de-briefing concluded and everyone but Shawn and Michael O'Leary remained behind. Morrison asked Crawford to have a seat.

"Shawn," Marshal Morrison began, "In the past 72 hours, there has been a rash of gruesome murders in the Sydney Suburbs that have everyone more than puzzled. Coincidentally, they started the day after you, Emily and Nathan returned from your narrow escape from Third Crusade warriors in the year 1197. Prior to the deaths in the Sydney area, three of our own maintenance personnel here at the base were found headless on the beach. They were discovered the morning after you and the others landed the afternoon before. A normal morning muster took place and the three airmen, two men and a woman, were found missing.

"At 0700 hours, the Sydney Police arrived and asked the sentries to talk with me about an 'episode' that occurred that morning. I was shocked at learning of the death of the airmen whom I was told were discovered a half hour earlier on the beach by ground crews starting their daily beach maintenance. The victims' heads were found washed up on the shore more than a half mile away from where their bodies were located. Each neck had what appeared to be puncture marks at the same spot below the left ear. "Naturally, the police came to us because they were our own people. I'd like you and Emily to go over to the Morgue at the Sydney Hospital and take a look at the condition of the remains. I know that you've just returned from the year 2017, but this viewing has an immediate priority. When you and Emily return, I want you find either Michael or me. Are there any questions?"

"No, Ma'am. Emily and Jolie are most likely in the outer office and waiting us to get through with our meeting. I'll pull Emily aside and fill her in on the details. We'll get back to either of you as soon as possible."

Shawn left and saw Emily speaking with Jolie. At the same time, the phone rang at Airman Coffill's desk. It was the Base Commander. She instructed Madelyn to have Jolie come back into her office. Coffill hung up the phone and walked over to where Shawn, Jolie and Emily were seated on a plush comfortable divan. She asked Jolie if she could have a further word with Marshal Morrison before they left for the afternoon. Madelyn walked her over to the Commander's closed door, politely knocked and showed Jolie into the room. Coffill closed the door and walked back to her desk.

In the interim, Shawn was in the process of briefing Emily about what he had just learned a few moments before. Emily listened passively and without emotion. Nothing ever surprised the 12-year-old girl. She followed Crawford outside the building and to a waiting car that Michael O'Leary had immediately requested for their brief trip into Sydney.

Shawn jumped behind the wheel as Emily had beaten him to the passenger side. She didn't put her seat belt on. Shawn looked over at her and she merely smiled and looked ahead. Crawford shrugged and drove off.

When they arrived at the Hospital, there was no one around outside the building. They walked in the front sliding doors and found the hallways empty. Shawn thought that this was more than a little strange and Emily stopped suddenly. She put her arm up to Crawford's chest to stop him from going any farther. It was deathly quiet.

They heard the screams coming from the opposite end of the hallway. Shawn raced to the end and turned left down a shorter walkway before turning right into a large open area with chairs placed along the walls. Emily was right behind him and was clutching a bronze-colored Medallion that hung from her neck on an equally old antique-looking bronze chain. She not only told Crawford to stop where he was, but commanded him to do so. The screaming had just then stopped.

Emily took the lead and proceeded to a closed door halfway down the corridor. She faced the door and signaled for Shawn to remain where he was. Emily opened the door.

Inside, she found a woman in Nurse uniform lying face down in her own blood. Her neck was nearly severed with muscles barely keeping her head attached to her torso. Emily looked up at the ceiling and saw that a vent cover had been removed. Shawn heard some scurrying above as if an animal had somehow got into the ceiling and was intent on getting away.

Emily motioned for Shawn to leave the room. The floor was washed with blood from the victim's torso. The red fluid continued to pump grotesquely from the body until it slowly stopped. Crawford started to leave the room when his foot slipped on the floor's gory mess. He fell to one knee as both of his hands kept him from falling altogether. With his fingers and palms, covered in the corpse's blood, he quickly recovered to follow Emily into the large foyer.

They continued down the hallway until they came to the cafeteria on the right. No lights were on and the door was slightly ajar. Emily told Shawn to follow her into the large luncheon area. When she turned on the lights, the sight inside was overwhelming.

There were bodies everywhere. One couldn't walk without stepping on an appendage of one of the victims lying bloodied on the floor. The copper-like odor of blood permeated the room. There must have been at least 30 bodies, all in various positions of dismemberment. The majority watched Shawn and Emily with eyes devoid of life. The horror of it all was unimaginable.

Emily, once again, viewed the entire scene dispassionately. Crawford motioned for the girl to exit the room. As they did, Shawn was attacked by a tall black hooded figure with a tall ebony cane. Emily immediately clutched at her Medallion and pulled it forward in the direction of what appeared to be a Demon. "You thought you could get rid of me back in 1197, didn't you Crawford? It's my turn to take revenge on you and to take back the Medallion held by that puny little girl. When I'm through with you, Crawford, you will not die, but will become one of my ageless minions!"

The Demon took his cane that immediately transitioned into a lethal blade. Emily resolutely stepped forward with the ancient Medallion in her right hand. As the Demon swung its cane at Shawn's head, Emily rushed forward with the Medallion held firmly at arm's length and pushed it against the Demon's chest. The timing couldn't have been better. Had Emily not interceded as she did, the cane-like device would have taken off Crawford's head. The dark figure dropped its blade immediately to the floor as Shawn had crouched to avoid the blow.

The Demon howled in excruciating pain. As it reeled back, it attempted to wrest the Medallion from Emily's possession. She had stepped backward once applying the surface of the Medallion to its chest and the Demon clutched at nothing but air. Seeing that it could not take the ancient metallic device from the girl, it ran into the large foyer and hurled itself through the glass to the outside. Once out of the building, it knelt for a moment and looked back at Crawford and Emily. An evil smile creased his lips and he vanished in a haze of red vapor.

Shawn, who had recovered to his feet, looked immediately to Emily to check to see if she was alright. Sensing Crawford's thought, Emily nodded once and said, "We need to go back to the Base now, Shawn, to warn the Marshal as to what we just witnessed here. Are you OK?" Crawford didn't need to be told twice to leave the Hospital building. They jumped into their military vehicle and raced back to the Base.

THE DILEMMA

As they sped out of the Hospital Emergency area, Crawford made a call back to the Sydney Police. He outlined what he and Emily had experienced, giving them the Cliff Notes regarding the gruesome experience. He hung up and called Morrison's office to tell her that they were on their way back to the Base. He would brief both her and Michael O'Leary after they arrived. She told him that there had been further atrocities at the Base Hangar while they were gone. She and O'Leary would meet them both at the Hangar site when they arrived back to the Base.

Shawn flashed his credentials to the Gate Guard and continued on to the Hangar. Emily had said nothing other than one word, 'Kennebunk' as they pulled up to an abrupt stop behind medical ambulances and a fleet of Base Air Police. Crawford looked at her briefly and exited the vehicle.

Morrison and O'Leary came over to them and informed both as to what had happened inside the aircraft structure. The two Airmen inside the Hangar who had assisted them upon their return to the Base were found horribly mutilated. Their heads had been torn off of their torsos and flung against the Hangar wall. Emily asked to view the scene of the murders and was allowed to enter. She walked calmly over to where medical personnel surrounded the corpses and politely asked if she could see the remains. The technicians fanned out to allow the girl access to the bodies.

She took the sheets off of both deceased Airmen, knelt between them, and studied them for several moments. She then got up and walked over to Morrison, O'Leary and Crawford. Emily looked at each of them for several moments before speaking.

"Shawn, tell us what you experienced as you climbed into the back of the ambulance at Jolie's murder scene. Please think about all details and any anomalies that come to mind. Don't leave anything out, please."

"Well, it's as I described previously. I talked the ambulance driver into letting me get into the back area where Jolie's body was. Through The Entity's intervention, I grabbed her arm and she was revived with a start. She was perplexed by her situation in the vehicle and I re-assured her that all was OK. After very few moments, The Entity transported us through the Gateway and into the F-193B Leopard where Nathan and Emily were.

"Wait a minute, there was something very strange that occurred as we transitioned from Kennebunk into the Fighter. A dark-colored breeze filtered into the back of the vehicle. It was almost like a mini-cloud of air had rushed in. Just before we 'jumped', I felt a brief very cold chill. And then, we were in the Leopard flying at altitude with Nathan at the controls."

"Emily," Morrison asked, "Did you notice anything when Shawn and Jolie appeared in the Fighter?"

"I sensed something, almost an additional presence aboard the aircraft. I said nothing to the others as Jolie was still in shock from her episode back in Maine. I didn't want to create a panic that something was not quite right aboard the Leopard. I wanted to talk with Shawn about it, but the right time didn't present itself."

"Well, there seems to be some connection to what you both experienced in the ambulance and the aircraft. Emily, could it have been something like a malevolent presence, or anything you have experienced previously in your time travels?" O'Leary asked.

"Yes, that is more than possible, even probable at this point, especially after seeing the bodies of those two Airmen. Their condition speaks to how Evil 'consumes' worldly beings. I'm certain that, if this is a case of Demonic intrusion, these two poor Airmen were attacked quickly. Their deaths were not swift. I'm positive that if, what we are talking about, that a Demon is here at the Base, the killing will not stop, slow down, but will escalate.

"What Shawn and I experienced at the Hospital was obviously a separate event. If I'm correct, we not only have one Demon to contend with, but two at-large," she confessed. At that moment, an Airman came over to their group and asked Morrison to take a call from the Sydney Police Chief.

'This is Marshall Morrison, Chief. What do you have for me?" Allison answered.

"Sir Shawn's call about the horrific occurrence was substantiated. Not only so, but the Officers and Medial Teams that arrived on the scene were found terribly mutilated by their vehicles when additional police personnel had arrived on the scene. Marshal, can you give me any information as to what we are dealing with here?" Chief McIntyre asked.

"Chief, I am sending both Sir Shawn and Emily, our Consultant, to you right away. Are you still at the Hospital?"

"No, we are proceeding to a location in the suburbs. Let me give you the address and they can meet us there," McIntyre responded.

Morrison relayed the phone message to Crawford and Emily. Both returned to their military sedan and left the area. It took them 10 minutes to get to the Chief's location. They parked behind an Ambulance with its emergency lights flashing. Two squad cars were on the opposite side of the street and blocking traffic from entering the block. By-standers were milling around on the opposite curbing from the home. Uniformed officers were stationed outside and ensuring that no one could gain access to the building. Crawford started to get out of the car, but Emily took hold of his arm and stopped him from opening up his side of the door. "Shawn, stay in the vehicle. Let's wait a moment. Something is about to happen outside this home," she insisted.

Just as she finished speaking, two bodies, one following the other, were thrust through the outside door with such force that they traveled 10 feet in the air and hit two of the trees in the front yard with incredible force. One of those lying bloodied on the ground was Chief McIntyre. Shawn recognized the other as the Coroner. By-standers began screaming in horror from across the way. Police officers raced to the front door and pushed their way into the home's foyer. Then, two shots were fired inside and then everything went quiet within the building.

Emily passively opened the passenger door of the vehicle and walked slowly up the walkway by-passing the severed heads without notice. Shawn was two steps behind her and warning the girl not to go inside without him.

Emily ignored Crawford completely while pulling the bronze-colored Medallion from beneath her outer clothing. They entered the home with Emily in the lead.

The three officers who had rushed in were scattered like rag dolls one atop the other in a corner just inside the living room. Their eyes stared vacantly upward as if they were accusing Emily for what had happened. A door in the back slammed shut and leading to the backyard area of the house. The girl walked calmly out of the living room and into the kitchen area that led to the outside. No one was there. However, on the wall above was written the words in blood, 'Emily, the Medallion is MINE!' The night was just beginning. The 'writing' on the wall served as a warning to Emily that further events would occur until she surrendered the ancient Medallion in her possession.

More uniforms arrived on the scene as Shawn and the girl left the home. A Detective told Shawn to remain for the moment until the house was cleared. A Police Sergeant immediately appeared from within and informed the detective of the bloodied bodies inside. Further backup was radioed in while Officers on the street attempted to calm the residents. In the interim, the severed heads on the front lawn were immediately covered over with blankets taken from the closest squad car. Moments later, a Police Helicopter arrived circled overhead. Communication between Ground and Air was taken over by a Sydney Police Corporal, a backup Pilot himself.

Shawn did all of the talking to the Detective while Emily stood serenely close by. When the Detective had received as much information as possible, they were allowed to head back to the Base with the caveat that more questions would most likely be asked within the next 24 hours.

When they both got in the military sedan, Shawn looked over at Emily who returned his gaze. "Shawn, I understand. We not only have one Demon to deal with, the one we brought back with us from the year 1197, but also the Demon that found its way into the rear of the Kennebunk Ambulance and then into the Leopard. We have a dilemma on our hands and, that is, how do we eliminate both 'Black Entities' in the Sydney without causing a wide spread panic throughout the City?"

It was close to 0200 hours when they returned to the Base. Shawn's Wife, Christine, and his two temporal Children, Christoper and Colette, were there waiting for him. Christine had got word of the murders through Shawn's best Friend, Admiral J. Hunter King, following a call to him by Michael O'Leary. King was present when Shawn and Emily returned. Also present, was another long-time Friend, Commodore Alberto 'Bob' Jesus Gonzales. Bob and Shawn had flown OH-58D Kiowa Helicopters in South America and later during the African States conflict. King had been instructed in the fine 'art' of rotary-wing flight, while Gonzales was Chief Instructor for all Rotary-Wing Instruction for military pilots. Bob was also proficient in the F-42A Tiger Shark and F-193B Leopard Advanced Stealth Fighter Aircraft.

Christine and Shawn's Children raced over to the sedan just as it stopped on the Base tarmac. Since returning from the Kennebunk Mission, Shawn had not even a chance to call his Family that he had returned. Christine gave him a huge hug and then punched him in the arm. Christopher and Colette merely smiled as they told him that they were glad to have him back.

Marshal Allison came over with O'Leary, King and Gonzales. The first question was to Emily. "Can we defeat this Thing? More importantly, are there two of them running around now in the City of Sydney? Please give me your best assessment."

"Shawn and I have talked about this very thing. Yes, I do believe that there are two Demons creating these two separate murders. The only method to overcome both is through containment. To achieve that status, they both must be neutralized with my Medallion. I see no other way at this point."

"Alright, Emily. I want you, Shawn, Hunter, and Bob to get your heads together and come up with a strategy as to how we are going to accomplish this. I am giving you four hours. Report back to me or Michael what your plan of attack is going to be. We're 'on the clock' in terms of stopping any more demonic events." With that, Allison Morrison and

Michael O'Leary went over to the Regional Police who had just arrived.

Shawn told the others to join him in the Headquarters Conference Room on the second floor of the Administration Building. As they resolutely walked the short distance, they could feel the fear emanating from the nearby Airmen.

Once inside, Shawn sat at the head of the large oak wood table. He motioned for Emily to sit to his right. Admiral King was seated to his left and Bob to Hunter's left. Crawford looked at each individual present finally resting his eyes on Emily. She had this far-away look on her face. She then looked over at the others and said to Shawn, "I know how I can overcome both of these Evil Entities.

She outlined her plan. They were not pleased with it, especially Shawn. The intent was to make Emily vulnerable and have the Demons come to her. She insisted this was the only way to stop their carnage. Emily recognized that the Seat of Power in Australia was what Evil wanted to conquer and so their plan would originate in the Capitol Building and in the House Chambers.

Shawn asked Emily that she was sure and that there was no other way to annihilate this Evil intrusion into Sydney, and ultimately into the Continent itself. She replied in the negative and that they should proceed to the Seat of Power immediately. Crawford noted that she was clutching firmly the Ancient Medallion to her chest.

Shawn informed Morrison as to what they were attempting to do. The Marshal was dubious at best, but had to rely on Emily's knowledge and drive of Evil to attain consummate power. It took them less than 10 minutes to reach the Capitol Building. There was no movement anywhere. Ironically, the front two huge doors leading into the Building were wide open.

Crawford, King, and Gonzales didn't like it. Emily looked Shawn squarely in the eye and told him that he and the others were to wait for her at the bottom of the steps.

Without a further word, the girl climbed the 14 steps to the Capitol doors. She entered into a mass of blackness. Crawford started to follow her in but King held him back. "This is her moment, Shawn. There is nothing more than any of us can do. Trust in Emily."

The young girl walked resolutely ahead through the foyer and to the balcony that looked overhead to the lower Chambers. She stopped briefly and surveyed the darkened Hall below her. Emily felt the Demons' presence, but did not hesitate to take the side stairway leading downward to the floor below. When she reached the bottom step, she hesitated briefly when a foul stench emanated from the center Hall. She continued walking forward to the central dais in front of the Chamber seats. Emily sat down in the ornate chair that looked down on the many desks and seats below her, and waited.

The Evil presence was nearly overwhelming. The girl sensed their location to be just overhead, but not quite in the balcony area. She looked upward to the left and then right and saw the two Demons descending slowly on each side of her. Emily took out the Ancient Medallion from around her neck and held it upward at arm's length directly in front of her.

As the Evil Ones stopped their descent on three feet on either side of the girl, the Demon to her left bellowed to the Other, "I will have that Medallion!!"

"You will never possess it. You are too weak! You allowed this tiny girl to overcome your stupidity in the year 1197. The Medallion will be forever mine!"

Both Demons stretched out their arms in the direction of the other. The whole Building quivered violently as if an earthquake had suddenly struck the area. Bolts of Laser-like lightning consumed them both, and Emily in the middle. Within the intensity of the light sat Emily. She was encased with a pale blue bubble that covered her from head to foot.

As the Demons struggled to wrest power from the other, Emily turned first to the Evil One on the left and quickly to the Other Demon on the right. Their Laser-like beams were immediately absorbed by the Medallion and quickly reversed to hit both Demons in the chest. They howled simultaneously as their bodies dissolved into ash. And then, absolute and very remarkable silence.

Shawn and the others out front waited anxiously for what would happen next. Emily came walking out the front doors and clutched the Medallion. The metal was glowing a rich bronze color as she stepped down onto the curb. She looked at Shawn before collapsing into his arms.

THE AFTERMATH

A few days later, Shawn, Bob, Emily, and Jolie climbed aboard the F-193B Leopard and took off looking for The Gateway. At 33,000 feet, the silence aboard the aircraft was broken suddenly by a Voice well known to Crawford.

"I am happy to see all of you once again. Emily, your heroics in Sydney have not gone unnoticed. For you to withstand the Demons' wrath was no easy task. I want you to know that you have a very special place in My Realm when the time comes. But, not for a long while, Emily. There are many more hurdles to overcome before we can eliminate the Evil in the World. Always know that I will be with you.

"And, Shawn, what more may I say that you are and always have been a very special Person to me. You also know that I have many more missions for you to undertake on My behalf. Safe journey back through My Doorway and to Kennebunk, Maine. Jolie, you are and always will be in safe hands with your Cousin, Shawn Crawford." And the, the Voice was gone.

Crawford looked over at Bob in the co-pilot's seat and said, "You and I both know that that Voice needs no introduction. Jolie, Emily, Bob and I will explain later. Just know that you will be safely home soon." Jolie O'Leary-Crawford then quietly went to sleep.

When Jolie awoke, she was lying on her couch that faced the huge glass window overlooking the ocean. She looked at her watch and wondered when Igor would be picking her up later that night to attend the play at the Ogunquit Play House. She still felt sleepy for whatever reason and fell back into a peaceful dream about Sydney, Australia.

AUTHOR BIOGRAPHY

Timothy James LTC O'Leary, III is a retired U.S. Army Lieutenant Colonel with 27 years of active duty and reserve service to his Country. Tim served a tour of duty in both Vietnam and the First Persian Gulf Wars. He is a graduate of the Defense Language Institute in Monterey, California where he earned a diploma in Italian Language training. Tim is a helicopter pilot with 2,200 hours of flight time in UH-1 and OH-58 aircraft with the United States Army. During Operation Desert Storm, Tim was a medevac pilot with the 217th Medical Battalion. His final tour of duty was Battalion Commander of the 286th Supply and Service Battalion.

He has a B.A. degree in Sociology and French, and holds a Master of Education and Educational Specialist degrees in Educational Administration and Supervision from Georgia Southern College. Tim was a Doctor of Education degree candidate at the University of Virginia in Educational Administration and Supervision. He also has one year of Spanish Language training at the University of Southern Maine in Portland. Tim taught foreign language and social studies in the Georgia public school system for three years and was an assistant principal at a secondary education school in Virginia.

Tim has run 13 marathons to include the Marine Corps in 1994 and Boston's 100th in 1996. He has been a baseball umpire for over 40 years and has officiated five Cal Ripken World Series. He currently serves on the Maine Little League District 6 Board as a Liaison Coordinator for the District Administrator. Tim played varsity baseball at Georgia Southern, semi-professional ball in Italy, and did a baseball tour with the European Continental Cavaliers Team in South Africa in 1971.

Tim has three children and three grandchildren. He and his Wife Lynn reside in Gorham, Maine.

OTHER BOOKS BY TIM O'LEARY

Tim O'Hara: His Life and Times

1
Tim O'Hara: The Early Years

2
The O'Hara Brothers

3
LT. Tim O'Hara

4
Tim O'Hara: A Tale of Two Lives:
A Shawn Crawford Adventure

5
Tim O'Hara: Red Sox Fighter Pilot

Shawn Crawford Adventures

1
The Gateway

2
Time Dimensions

3
The Dimensional Gateway

OTHER BOOKS BY TIM O'LEARY

4
The Assigner

5
Missions

6
Nathan

7
Christopher

8
Cdr. J. Hunter King

9
Warriors

10
Sancha

11
Knights

12
The Last War

13
Aruba

14
Dangerous Liaisons

OTHER BOOKS BY TIM O'LEARY

The Portal

The Entity's War

The Entity's Child

The Entity's Chosen

The Narragansett Trail

The Demons of Gotham

Joey

A Demon Tetrology

Witches and Vampires

FREEING KUWAIT: A SOLDIER'S MEMOIR

Nowhere To Run

Co-Authored Works of Tim O' Leary:

The Tasmanian Devil: A Feline Novella by Lynn Carol OLeary

Crying in Silence by Shelley Lynn O'Leary

www.ingramcontent.com/pod-product-compliance
Lightning Source LLC
LaVergne TN
LVHW041936070526
838199LV00051BA/2802